THE LUCKY LADY SALOON

(THE DEADMAN BOOK 6)

LINELL JEPPSEN

WOLFPACK
PUBLISHING
— EST 2013 —

The Lucky Lady Saloon

Paperback Edition
Copyright © 2020 Linell Jeppsen

Published in the United States by Wolfpack Publishing, Las Vegas

Wolfpack Publishing
6032 Wheat Penny Avenue
Las Vegas, NV 89122

wolfpackpublishing.com

Paperback ISBN 978-1-64734-690-4
eBook ISBN 978-1-64734-689-8

THE LUCKY LADY SALOON

PART ONE

1

1888

Thirteen-year-old, Stephanie Mack awoke with a start and studied the spider that lived above her bed in the wooden beams of the loft. It was a garden spider—both frightfully ugly with its beige shell-like body and long segmented legs, and achingly beautiful as it spun its web in the early dawn light.

Stephanie, better known as Sweetie, decided that as soon as she found time, she would bring the broom upstairs and remove the spider (yet again) to the Clematis vines on the west side of the house. She knew that soon the spider would hatch her progeny and long, fuzzy tentacles of hatched spider eggs would fall toward her face and body.

The girl shuddered at the thought and threw her covers back. Listening carefully, she tried to judge whether any of her father's friends were up and about yet. Not hearing anything besides a chorus of frogs outside and a few soft snores coming from her pa- Dean Mack- who slept on a cot in the hallway outside her bedroom door, she decided it was safe to head downstairs.

She got up from her bed and walked toward the pocket watch sitting on top of the chifforobe. 5:20, the watch announced. Sighing with relief, Sweetie knew she had time to feed the chickens, take their eggs, milk the cow, make coffee and prepare a fine breakfast for Pa and his buddies, before they even opened their eyes to the new day.

She got dressed and stepped into a small enclosed room, which had once served as a linen closet, but was now a locked and somewhat hidden exit from her bedroom, as her pa had taken to sleeping in front of her bedroom door. This had happened only recently – once her monthlies had begun to flow.

Sweetie wasn't sure why this had happened, or why she suddenly garnered her pa's suspicious scrutiny, but it had to do with becoming a woman. At least that was what her pa had said, red-faced and terse. It was times like this, Sweetie missed her ma the most. She loved her pa, but he knew almost nothing about being a girl, much less a girl's transition into womanhood.

Sarah, Sweetie's mother, had been the most feminine of ladies. Blue-eyed and fair-skinned, her dark brown hair curled into ringlets and her bosom smelled of roses. Sarah had transfixed the citizens of Fairwood County, and kept her wild young husband glued firmly by her side, until she was carried off by a virulent case of the bloody flux.

That was four years ago, and Sweetie missed her ma's

gay laugh, and gentle manners. She also missed Sarah's lessons. There were all the bookish things like primers, math books, maps, fiction and poetry. But, more importantly, it was life's personal lessons Sweetie missed the most.

If Sarah were still here, for example, she might be able to explain why those dang monthlies hurt so bad, and what to do with the ever-growing nubs on her chest. And, mainly, why all of her father's buddies had suddenly stopped looking at her with careless, comfortable comradery, and now studied her with caution, and shifty-eyed intensity.

Sweetie walked past her pa who was curled up like a shrimp on his cot and crept downstairs. She saw that only four of her pa's friends had decided to stay overnight. Two of them were stretched out in the living room and she could see that two more men were sleeping on the porch. One man, named Kevin Woolsey, was stretched out on the divan, mouth open and a drool of spit pooling on the sofa's upholstery.

She frowned and shook her head in exasperation. *How many times have I asked him to use a sheet before falling asleep on Ma's sofa?* she wondered. Still, even though Kevin's manners were sometimes uncouth, he was one of the few of her pa's friends she really trusted.

The only other man she trusted was her uncle, Jedediah Cummins, her mother's brother, who was sleeping in her pa's rocking chair in front of the woodstove. Older than Dean by a decade, Jed was fiercely protective of her, and tried as best he knew how to teach her about farming and animal husbandry.

He even, in his own clumsy way, tried to help her navigate a man's world as a woman. It was he who had suggested she tie one of her ma's old scarves around her chest to hide her budding breasts, and had fashioned some soft, medical bandages into pads to catch her menstrual flow. He had once had himself a wife and daughters and remembered some of what they were forced to endure every month.

He had also told her to keep clean- NO MATTER WHAT- and to never, ever wear talcum powder or rose water. "At least not here, at this time...d'ya hear me?" he had snarled one morning when she'd stumbled downstairs in her thin cotton nightshirt, sweaty from the summer heat, and reeking of healthy, young girl.

She had been appalled to see that the living room and kitchen were filled with men, young and old alike, who stopped and stared at her with hungry eyes, like coon dogs on the scent, and the air grew thick and heavy with thwarted desire.

Dean happened to be outside with a couple other men and didn't see what had happened but shortly after that, he had set his cot up outside her bedroom door, and Jed did his best to keep her hidden from her father's companions.

Sweetie grabbed the egg basket and pulled on a pair of her ma's old boots. Then, stepping outside, she saw the men sleeping on the front porch and her heart sank. The screen-door screeched like a banshee, no matter how many times she oiled the old springs that kept it closed against the flies and skeeters, and she winced as the younger of the two men opened one eye and gazed up at her with a lascivious grin.

"Well, hello there, Sweetie. Whatcha doin' up so early?" Pete Meadows drawled with a nasty leer.

"Goin' to fetch us some eggs for breakfast, that's all," she stammered, blushing. For some reason, Pete Meadows, whom she'd known for most of her life, suddenly scared the dickens out of her. She'd always thought of him as a friend, but he'd changed recently, making her feel stupid, clumsy and ill-at-ease.

Sweetie had never thought of herself as a beauty and, indeed, she wasn't by society's standards a pretty girl. She was tall and raw-boned like her father. Her face was angular, and her mouth was too wide. Her hair was, Sweetie reckoned, the color of a mud puddle and about as attractive. But she couldn't see in the mirror of her room that she was as graceful as a swan, and her high, freckled cheekbones and pointed chin were as winsome a sight as a new fawn in early summer.

Her eyes were her best feature. Although they were a bit small and round as pennies, they were as blue and soft as robin's eggs and framed by thick dark lashes. Even *she* was sometimes startled by how...colorful her orbs were, so she mostly kept them lowered and rarely made eye-contact with anybody besides her pa and uncle.

"Go back to sleep and leave the girl alone, Petey," Ed Meadow's snapped and Pete, with a long, meaningful wink, turned over and closed his eyes.

Sweetie, as if let loose of a cobra's deadly gaze, stepped off the porch and practically ran to the chicken coop, where she dropped the basket and clutched at her chest as if her heart might make free and fly away on its own, it was pounding so hard.

She took a few deep breaths, picked the wire basket up and started searching for new eggs.

2

Later that same year, Sweetie lay in her bed and studied the industrious spider which had, somehow, found its way back from the Clematis on the other side of the house. The spider that Sweetie had decided to call Millie, lay sleeping in a soft cocoon of her own making, and so did the girl who watched.

Sweetie had a heavy heart, and just wanted to stay in her bed forever, but she knew it was time to get up and face the day and whatever it had in store for her. But it was so hard, and fear filled her heart.

About six months earlier, two new friends of her pa's had come to stay. They were bad, bad men and no amount of wishing it weren't so could change Sweetie's mind. For the longest time, she had suspected that her father's friends were less than friends, and more like co-workers.

She had long denied the realization that her pa, along with the assortment of men who came to call and some-times stayed on for weeks and even months were crooks, but with the arrival of a man named Billy Drake and his sidekick, Edwardo Martinez- or Eddie Machete, she knew her suspicions were correct.

When she'd finally confronted her pa about it, he blew up with anger. "It don't make no never mind to you how I put food on the table, brat!" He hollered in her face, adding, "I could just send you off on yer own if you don't like it!"

Sweetie had read a book once about a whole family of kids who'd lost their parents and wandered the land, alone and afraid, grubbing for food and medicine, almost dying until they were finally saved by a kindly spinster.

Thinking back on how deeply that novel had frightened her, Sweetie ran to her angry father, howling with fear. "No, Pa! Please, it don't matter to me, okay? Just please, PLEASE don't send me away all on my own!"

Dean stared down at his daughter's tousled hair and felt what was left of his heart shrivel up in shame. "Now, now..." he murmured. "...don't fret, Sis, I ain't sending you nowhere."

Sweetie had stepped back to give her pa a tremulous smile when Jed stepped into the kitchen. He cleared his throat and said, "The way you two are carrying on, Billy and Eddie are bound to hear and put all of us away for good. So, shut up."

Dean stared at his brother-in-law. "Did they hear us, you think?"

Jed shook his head. "Nah, I don't reckon they did, they're out by the corral but we all got to be extra careful, okay?"

Dean nodded and stared at his daughter. "You're right, Sweetie. I didn't mean to, not really, but times were bad, and money was short after yer ma passed over. I went for some quick cash, but got us – all of us – involved with a bunch of criminals…" He wiped a sudden, unwelcome tear from his eye and plowed ahead. "Thing is, it's too late to back out now, especially since Billy D showed up. I had no idea that he was as evil a skunk as there ever was, and now he's calling the shots around here."

Gazing at Sweetie's stricken face he added, "I'm making plans, honey. Me and yer uncle both have got a plan to us get outta this fix. Meanwhile though, you gotta act like you don't know what's going on around here, okay? You gotta be as quiet as a mouse and stay outta sight as much as possible. It's dangerous for you."

Sweetie's bright blue eyes grew red and her freckles blazed like tiny bonfires across her nose and cheeks. "Do you think they want to hurt me?" she asked.

Dean shrugged. "Maybe not in the way you think, Sis, but yes; they would hurt you plenty if they could." He glared at her again. "Honestly, it might be better for you if you *did* head out. Maybe go to a girl's school far away from here."

"No, Pa!" Sweetie gasped but was interrupted when another voice filled the air. "What's this, then? You plan on sending this gal off to school, Mack?"

Both Dean Mack and Jedidiah jumped at the unwelcome words and heavy footsteps of Billy Drake. Drake was a huge man with long, red hair and small brown eyes. He had come to stay in late April and showed no sign of leaving.

He was heavy-handed, coarse and cruel to man and beast alike. He was also a quick gun – one of the quickest in the Northwest, Dean had heard to his dismay, and the minute he stepped inside Dean's house, he had taken over ownership.

It made no difference that Dean Mack owned the title free and clear and had built the house, barn and stables with his own two hands. Once Billy D moved in, Dean was forced to step back and make way for the new boss, or he and everyone he loved would suffer the consequences.

Billy looked Sweetie up and down and then stepped forward and took the girl's chin in his big paw. Looking into her pretty blue eyes, he shook his head, and said, "Nah. You won't be sending this one off, you hear? She's a good cook and keeps the place tidy enough."

He pinched her cheek so hard, Sweetie winced and tried not to weep. "Besides, we ain't got time to break us in another cook, do we? Someone who will keep his or her mouth shut – right?" His tone was reasonable, as if only *he* knew the real sound and sense behind his words.

Dean Mack trembled with rage but nodded. "I guess so," he replied and gestured with his eyes for Sweetie to make herself scarce.

Sweetie ran from the room but pulled up short by the door so she could hear the rest of the men's conversation. She heard her uncle Jed say, "I'm a decent cook, Billy. Did my share of chuckin' chow on a coupla different cattle drives. Why don't you let Sweetie move on, so she don't get hurt by what we're doing?"

His words made sense to Sweetie, of course, but then she heard a strangled gasp and felt a heavy thud. "My God! You killed him, Eddie! Why?" Dean groaned, and Sweetie flew back through the door and ran, screaming, to her beloved uncle's side.

Jed lay on his back groaning and digging his boot heels into the floorboards. A dense pool of blood was making its way from under his body and ran in rivulets toward the kitchen sink. He'd been stabbed in the back, and even as Sweetie watched, Jed's eyes grew fixed, he let out a long, shuddering breath and died.

The girl's world stood still for a moment and then she stared up at Edwardo. "You killed my uncle...over nothing!" At first, Sweetie's words were hushed but then her voice rose into a howl and she sprang up from the floor, and lunged toward the silent, leering Mexican with long, clawed fingers as stiff as nails.

Before Eddie even had a chance to react, Sweetie's fingernails reached his eyes and she dug in with the fury and focus of a cornered badger. "AIEEE!!!" the man screamed as he felt one of her claws lift his right eye from its socket. She would have pulled it right out of his head, but his knife hand took over.

Eddie Machete's big knife burned a path across Sweetie's face, and she sank to the floor with a gasp. At first, the blood running down her cheek seemed cold, and somewhat refreshing. But then, pain took over and she screamed as blood ran through her fingers, and down her neck.

"That's enough, goddammit!" Billy yelled and Eddie took a step back.

"She almost put my eyes out, Patron! Let me bathe in her blood – she's too ugly to live now, anyway!" Edwardo snarled and took another step in her direction, but Dean had finally gathered his wits and pointed his pistol at the furious Mexican.

"Take one more step and you'll be meeting yer maker right soon." Dean hissed.

Looking over at Billy, Edwardo silently asked for permission to dispatch the little wildcat, and her father for good, but Billy shook his head. "No, leave it alone Eddie. Just go outside and cool down, alright?"

Eddie glared but realized he still had two good eyes and his face was just a little scratched up. He spat at Dean, wiped his bloody knife off on Sweetie's skirt and stepped outside.

Dean and Billy stared down at the girl for a moment and then Dean asked, "Can you get someone to fetch my brother-in-law's body outside for buryin'? I need to tend to my girl right now."

Billy stared Dean in the eye, and then he said, "Sure. I'll do that. But remember this – you might not like it, but I'm the boss man around here now. Keep your mouth shut about this and don't go trying to make future plans without my say-so. I figure Eddie and I will be gone soon enough, but until then – you answer to me. Got it?"

***

Now, as Sweetie lay in her bed and dreaded the new dawning, she missed her ma, and her uncle and just wished, more than anything, that Billy Drake and Eddie Machete would dry up and blow away.

3

Sighing, she got out of bed and tried not to look in the mirror at the ragged, ugly scar that ran from the corner of her mouth to her right temple. Sweetie was not a vain girl, but the five-inch scar caused her great embarrassment and made her even more clumsy and self-conscious than she was before.

She ran a comb through her hair, did a little wash-up in the basin on top of the bureau and dressed for the day ahead. She could see her breath on the air and decided to wear two pairs of socks and an old knitted shawl over her dress. Then, she walked over to the window and looked outside.

Smiling slightly, Sweetie stared at the heavy frost gilding the grass, trees, horses' backs and outbuildings. Shaggy Manes! She thought with a pang of loss. The Mack's homestead was situated about fifty miles north of Spokane, Washington Territory, and pine trees, blue spruce, low-lying hills and far-flung mountains surrounded the farm. Sweetie and her ma had often taken advantage of the mountain's bounty, like fresh and icy-cold Brook trout in the spring, Shaggy Mane and Morrel mushrooms in the early days of autumn and Huckleberries in the heat of summer. Oh, how she missed those day and, especially, her dear mother!

It was still quite early, and for once, the house was empty. Only a man named Steven Kingston, and Eddie Machete were here at present, and they had made themselves comfortable in the barn loft. Sweetie screwed her lips up and spat on the floor in contempt. Then, she frowned at the mess, knelt and wiped the spittle up with her washrag.

She had an amazing thought – one that might make her pa smile and help get her mind off the fact that Billy D and quite a few men were expected back by nightfall. They were out on a "job" she knew, and she wondered if they would arrive in style with boastful laughter, plenty of vittles, new tack and grain for the horses, and cash to spare.

Or, would they be sullen and down-in-the-mouth, their desires thwarted, law dogs hot on their trail. Either way, she hoped to have her work done and be well hidden in her room by the time they arrived.

Making a snap decision, she stuck her head out the bedroom door and saw that her pa was not sleeping on his cot in the hallway, Shrugging, she thought, *oh well, what he don't know won't hurt him.*

Sweetie tip-toed down the stairs, put on her coat, grabbed a small gunnysack and headed outside to pick a peck of mushrooms for her pa's supper. The air was crisp and cold, but she could see that the sun was rising in a clear blue sky and knew that within a few hours the rising heat would erase the frost, like long-ago memories.

Looking about for watching eyes, she felt that the coast was clear and headed toward a pretty glade that graced a wooded hillside about a mile from the house. Blue jays darted about like winged sapphires, and bullfrogs thumped and hummed in the bull rushes.

Slowing down, Sweetie started searching the ground for the tell-tale cone-shaped mushrooms her pa loved so much. According to Dean there had once been a wildfire around these parts and apparently, the ash left over from the burnt timber promoted the mushrooms' growth.

She ambled along trying to let her eyes adjust and then – there they were! About a dozen fresh new mushrooms had risen up out of the frost, and Sweetie knelt and sawed each one off at ground level. Then, she gazed about and realized she was standing in the middle of a huge fungus-filled patch! Sweetie grinned and set-to. Working hard, she was suddenly happy, happier than she'd been in ages.

Sweetie picked and picked and then she heard a branch snap and ducked in instant fear. *Is it a bear?* she wondered and knew that she should have brought her pa's old shotgun. Now, after all, was the time of year that any self-respecting bear would be stocking up on autumn forage before its long winter slumber.

Lifting her head slowly, oh so slowly, Sweetie gazed

about looking for a black, or worse, brown bear but saw nothing close by. Sighing with relief, she started to stand back up but heard another loud cracking noise and spun around to see her pa making his way through the woods about 500-yards away.

He was looking over his shoulder in a sly, furtive manner and every move he made seemed to scream that he was afraid of being caught. She was going to run over and show him her bounty, but Sweetie knew that she, herself, wasn't supposed to be out and about by herself and she didn't want to make her father angry.

So, she crouched as low to the ground as she could and watched as her father felt around behind a large fallen log and pulled out one of their shovels. He had apparently hidden it there earlier and was set on using it now. He took another long look around to make sure he wasn't being watched, and then he started to dig.

He dug furiously, stopping often to see if his actions were being observed, then he picked up a large carpet bag. *Ma's, carpetbag!* Sweetie thought resentfully.

Dumping the bag inside the freshly dug hole, Dean proceeded to fill it back in, and then take great pains to hide the hole's presence. "What's he hiding?" Sweetie whispered, and then thought, *I bet it's money!*

Once that thought entered her mind, Sweetie knew that it was true. Pa was acting too sneaky for that bag to contain anything but ill-gotten booty. She sighed and wondered if her pa, or for that matter, she herself would survive this entanglement with these no-good crooks. She watched as her pa brushed the area clean with a long pine branch, and then tossed a bunch of pinecones around for more cover.

Then she caught movement out of the corner of her eye. Eddie Machete was making his way slowly through the woods, heading straight for Dean. Not knowing what else to do, Sweetie gave out a shout and ran toward her pa with a huge, phony grin on her face. "Lookit, Pa! Lookit how many I got!" For all the world as if she and Dean had been picking mushrooms together this whole time.

Dean started and stared in shock, but catching sight of the tall, ugly Mexican man headed his way, he smiled in return and said, "Good job, Sis! You sure done better than I did!" Then he headed her way with long strides- laughter in his voice, but naked fear in his eyes that only she could see.

Sweetie noticed beads of nervous sweat dotting her pa's forehead, but he pulled off his part in the play flawlessly. Stooping down, he ruffled through her mushrooms and for effect, actually scolded her for picking them before their time, and threw a couple of them on the ground in disgust.

At which time, Eddie showed up and stared at the two of them with beady, suspicious eyes. "Whatchu got there?" he asked.

"My daughter and I decided to pick mushrooms for the boys' dinner tonight. They only come out after a thaw, and the timing was right," Pa answered, while Sweetie trembled with fear.

Eddie studied them and the mushrooms in the sack,

and then shrugged disdainfully. "Ugly, horrible things" he snickered. "Just like you, puta."

Sweetie blushed to the roots of her hair but sighed in relief as he turned around and made his way back from where he came. Dean, watching the outlaw make his way back to the ranch sighed in relief as well.

"Good thinking, Sweetie," he murmured and tipped his hat back to swipe the sweat away from his face. "Let's head back."

They took off walking, keeping some distance between themselves and Billy's right-hand man, but close enough that Eddie could see they were following.

"How long were you watching?" Dean asked.

Sweetie winced, but answered, "I was there before you, Pa. I knew that the shaggies were out and thought to give you a treat. Sorry..."

"Yeah, you were wrong to go out on yer own, but you saved my bacon, that's fer sure. Can you remember where I put the bag?"

She swallowed. "Yes, I think so."

He nodded. "That's good. Never forget that it's there, okay? If worse comes to worst, you sneak back and dig it up fer yourself. It's enough money for you to start over fresh if'n you need it. Hopefully, Billy D and his gang will move on, and we'll be set up, but just in case..."

They were approaching the corral fence and Eddie had turned around to watch their arrival. "I gotta go, honey. Get inside and put on a good spread. Then head upstairs. I don't want you around when the boys get back."

She nodded and tried to ignore the sight of her pa sidling up to the Mexican bandit like a whipped dog.

4

Three weeks later, Sweetie's world came crashing down. The gang, most of whom had been gone more often than not, was back now and the mood around the farm was grim. Sweetie was not privy to the men's activities when they left the farm, but she was smart enough to read the signs of discontent and fear in most of the men's faces.

Billy Drake was filled with rage, and most of that anger seemed to be aimed at two of his closest companions, Kevin Woolsey and Pete Meadows. The men were feeling the brunt of Billy's anger and were treated to numerous sarcasms and the worst of the many endless chores needed to keep a ranch like this in good working order.

The tension was palpable, the culprits were resentful and sullen. Eddie was a constant, scowling threat and worse, Dean, although nowhere near whatever trouble had occurred on the gang's most recent trip out, was on the receiving end of Billy's wrath. Before they left, Billy had told Dean to stay home and mind the farm along with

Edwardo while they were gone, so whatever mistakes had taken place along the way were in no way Dean's fault. Still, it was Sweetie's pa that Billy took his rage out on.

If things weren't already tough enough for Dean Mack – who had lost his older brother to Billy and Eddie, had his farm wrestled out from under him and was basically being held hostage, along with his daughter, in his own home while the gang rode roughshod over the territory – things were now twice as bad. Not a day went by that Billy's fist did not find a way to give Dean a cuff on the face or a kick in the pants.

This morning, a sheriff out of Spokane County had shown up at the gate leading to the ranch and demanded to talk to the owner. Billy and Eddie had stood on either side of Dean who was standing just inside the front door, trying to gather his wits, when Eddie hauled off and hit him so hard in the kidney, he sank to his knees and vomited in agony.

Billy hissed, "You better send that law dog packing right quick or your daughter will suffer your ineptitude, got it?"

Dean shuddered and nodded his head. He looked back at his daughter, who was standing by the kitchen door with her hand over her mouth, trembling with fear and said, "You go upstairs, sis. Lock the door."

Eddie started to grumble but Billy said, "Oh, for pity's sake, leave it alone, Eddie. We got enough trouble without you making a fuss over that stupid little girl again."

Eddie backed away and Dean watched as Sweetie ran

up the stairs. Then, he faced the front door. He was still seeing stars, but he climbed to his feet and staggered outside. The sheriff watched his approach with narrowed eyes, and called out, "Name's Sheriff Hilton, out of Spokane Falls. What took you so long to answer my call?"

Dean winced. "Pleased to meet you, sir. My name's Dean Mack, and my back's all stove in. Horse kicked me about a week ago, and I've been a-bed ever since tryin' to recover."

The sheriff grimaced in sympathy. "Yup, happened to me too, a long time ago. One of my pa's mules knocked the starch right outta me. Could hardly walk for a month." The man leaned over and spat a mouthful of brown juice on the ground while Dean squirmed in discomfort, aware that over a half a dozen eyes were trained on his every move.

Finally, when the sheriff stayed silent, Dean asked, "So, what can I do fer ya, Sheriff?"

The sheriff turned around in his saddle and gazed back at the now open gate where young Pete Meadows stood by with a smirk as big as his hat plastered on his mug. Turning back to look down at Dean, Hilton wore a frown. "Just stopping by to see if you've noticed anything interesting around these parts lately. You know, strangers lurking about causing trouble. Figured I'd gather some info from the locals – innocent bystanders. Then I run into that young scamp guarding your gate…it surely made me wonder if I'd found the rascals I've been looking for."

Dean's blood ran cold. The sheriff's instincts ran truer than he could have known, and he thought, *Gawd, Pete is as stupid as a goat. No wonder Billy is pissed at him!*

He smiled a little, though, for the sheriff's benefit. "Sorry, sir. That's my neighbor's son, Pete. His pa sent him over to help out around here until I get my boots under me again. That kid has never been known for his manners, and right now he's doubly mad, because he's sparkin' a new girl over west of here, and spendin' time with me is takin' time away that he could be spendin' with her. Sorry, though, if'n he was too rude."

Dean watched as Sheriff Hilton chewed on that news, and added, "But, in answer to yer question, no sir. I ain't seen nor heard of any strangers around these parts. 'Course, I stay home most of the time and well, the last few days I've been out of commission entirely."

Hilton studied the house and yard around the barn. "Got quite a few horses, don't cha?" he asked Dean.

Starting to tremble with fear at the certain knowledge that his daughter would be the first to suffer and die if this meeting didn't go well, Dean smiled. "Yes. Well, temporarily at least. These horses are already sold to the cavalry outpost, about ten miles away from here. I'm expectin' a couple of those Army boys to come and fetch them sometime this week. Sure could use the money – although I ain't got the energy to spend any right now."

Hilton seemed to buy Dean's lies, although his small brown eyes skittered here and there, as if he could sense the evil gaze staring holes in his body. In truth, Race Hilton was feeling downright stupid for coming out here all alone. He had sent his deputies ahead to neighboring farms, meaning for all of them to meet up later to compare notes, never expecting to run into trouble this far out of town.

Now, seeing the naked fear in Mack's eyes and catching a glimpse of raw metal gleam darkly from an upstairs window, Hilton knew he was in BIG trouble if he didn't make his way out of here as soon as possible. The sheriff smiled slightly, tipped his hat and said, "Well, that's good you ain't seen anything out of the ordinary. If I were you, though, I would lock your place up. There's a bad gang of outlaws making trouble around the Spokane Falls area. I know that's a ways off from here, but they like to steal other folks homes when they decide to lay low and I'd hate to see you become a victim of their hijinks..."

Turning his horse around, Hilton lifted his hat a little and said, "I'll be taking off now – I gotta meet the deputies who are just around that there bend in the road. If'n I don't show up soon, they'll be forced to come and find me." He grinned, adding, "I'd hate to roust you outta bed again, when they come a knocking looking for their wayward sheriff!"

Hilton knew that talking about his deputies was a risk but hoped that the idea of reinforcements just down the road might keep a bullet from finding his back as he rode away.

Dean, almost collapsing in relief, called out, "Hope you find your outlaws soon, sir!"

Hilton grinned. "Oh, we will, Mister Mack. We surely will." Then, the sheriff spurred his gelding past young Pete, who had to step back out of the way of the horse's flying hooves and was forced to eat the man's dust as he rode off down the road and out of sight.

As he walked back toward the house, Dean couldn't decide what to do. He was pretty sure that no one inside the house could have heard his and the sheriff's conversation, but he wasn't so sure about what, if anything, Pete might have overheard. Also, he wasn't sure where Kevin Woolsey was hiding – if he was in the barn, he would have heard every word they spoke.

By the time he stepped up on the stoop, Dean had decided to tell the truth. Letting Billy know that the sheriff was not alone, might just push him to pack up and leave, and wouldn't that be just fine! Wiping a trembling hand across his mouth, Dean took a deep breath and opened the front door...

5

The minute Dean stepped inside the house he knew something was wrong. He wasn't sure what, or why every hair on his head suddenly stood on end, but he knew without a doubt that Sweetie was in trouble. Heart pounding, Dean called out, "Hey, where is everybody? Sweetie, come down here!"

The living area and kitchen were empty, but he heard a muffled voice from upstairs and Dean immediately ran up the steps, two and three at a time. He saw Kevin gathering up some gear and piling it on the landing and asked, "Hey, where is everybody?"

Kevin shrugged and looked away, shame coloring his face and darkening his eyes. Dean's heart lodged in his throat and he turned to face Sweetie's bedroom door. He saw that his cot had been pushed aside and at the same moment, heard a muffled shriek. Taking two long steps he rushed to the door and turned the doorknob, only to find it locked.

Hearing snickers and muted laughter, Dean understood what was happening to his girl and with a mighty lunge he threw his shoulder at the door and almost stumbled to the bedroom floor as the wood gave away easily. Standing stock-still, he saw that Edwardo was heaving away at Sweetie's prone and tender body, even as his huge palm covered her mouth and nose so tightly her cheeks were turning red and her eyes bugged from lack of oxygen.

From the corner of his eyes, he saw that all the gang members, except for Kevin and Peter were ringing the room and watching lasciviously. He also saw that Pete's father, Ed Meadows, had his dungarees down around his hips and was readying himself to take the next turn at his girl's innocence.

Red-hot fury filled his soul at the violation, both of his daughter and himself. Granted, he had let the gang get a foothold in his hearth and home, but he had been tricked by Billy's charming manners into thinking he was part of *something* – something that could maybe make him rich and allow him to secure his daughter's future. *Something* to fill the deep and terrible void that had entered his life after his beloved wife passed. Now, he knew himself to be the worst of all fools.

"Rapist!" Dean snarled. If he had been able to use his pistol, Eddie Machete would be bleeding out now and gasping his last, but about three weeks earlier, Billy had demanded that Dean disarm, leaving only the most willing participants in the gang's activities armed. Still, a furious red haze filled his eyes as Edwardo jerked and heaved over his daughter's white thighs. He took the knife he'd taken to wearing on the sly and leapt on Edwardo's back, sinking the blade deep inside the man's kidney. Then, even as Eddie screamed and writhed, Dean stabbed again and again as panicked shouts filled the room, and hands seized his arms.

Sweetie stared up into her Pa's stricken eyes as he was dragged off the bed, and she heard him murmur, "I'm sorry, Sweetie, so sorry." Then, she had to look away because the man pinning her to the bed gave out a ragged gasp and collapsed, essentially cutting off her ability to breathe. She gasped and gurgled and tried to push at the rapist's body to crawl out from under the dead weight.

Then, she stopped and stared as a single shot rang out with a deafening BOOM! She saw a small, tidy hole in her Pa's forehead and gazed, mesmerized, at the wide swath of blood and brain matter painting the white-washed wall behind Dean's body. She opened her mouth to scream out her pain and loss, but a quiet voice filled the sudden silence.

Peter stood in the doorway studying the mess. "Uh, boss? Um, I heard that sheriff has a posse with him. I heard him say they was camped out just down the road...thought you'd want to know." His eyes looked like black holes as he saw the blood-soaked body on Sweetie's bed and the dead, staring eyes of her father.

Billy still stood with his pistol smoking in his hand, staring down at Dean Mack and then over at his right-hand man, Edwardo Martinez. Eddie looked like nothing more than a punctured sack – all his mighty strength depleted, the furious vigor animating the living man gone and reduced to nothing more than dead meat. Then, as if waking from a dream, Billy shook his head and turned toward Pete who was now wringing his hat in his hands. "What's that you say, Pete?" he asked in a vague way.

"That sheriff, boss! I heard him say he had some deputies with him, and they were just down the road and around the bend. I don't know – maybe he was lying, but he sounded dead serious to me. Just thought you should know, sir, that's all."

Suddenly, as though he'd been slapped in the face, the blank expression left Billy's eyes. He holstered his pistol, stood up straight, and hollered, "Kevin, you got that gear packed up yet?"

"Yes, sir, it's ready to go," came the reply from the upstairs hallway.

Sweetie had taken advantage of the men's lack of attention and crawled into the narrow space between her bed and the wall. She was eyeing the floorboards and wondering if she could somehow fit her body into the three floorboards, she'd loosened to store her keepsakes, when she heard Kevin's words.

Her heart stood still as she understood that she was about to die. Billy wouldn't want to leave her alive and a witness to his crimes. She knew there was no way she could fit into the hidey-hole, it was far too shallow, and she understood that she would be easy pickin's for Billy's next bullet. Her heart pounded in dread, and before she could utter the Lord's Prayer for deliverance, she heard Billy shout, "Come on, boys, it's time to fly!"

Sweetie looked on in shock as she realized that Billy had, somehow, forgotten all about her; attributing no more time and thought to her now than if she was a bothersome fly that had been shooed away. Too bewildered to feel relief, she watched as Pete's father glanced in her direction, hitched up his pants and strode out the door after Billy.

Heartsick and bleeding she heard the men pick up their gear from outside her door and scramble down the stairs. After a few shouted commands, she listened as the men left the house. Then, she scrambled out from behind the bed and crept to the window. She saw the men saddle their horses and ride away – from her, her father Dean, and all the broken dreams they'd left in their passing.

Finally, as silence moved over her like a dense grey cloud, Sweetie Mack stared at Edwardo's fat bloody body, and at her father's sad, half-closed blue eyes. Then, she hung her head and wept.

6

Sweetie awoke with a gasp and a groan of pain. Opening her eyes slowly she peered about at the dim light in the room. *What time is it? Why is it so dark?* she wondered. She figured that her ordeal had begun in the morning hours...thinking back on it with horror, she *knew* it was about 10:00 a.m. that Billy and the rest of the gang had busted into her bedroom.

So, had she actually slept the whole day away...her slumber made more comfortable with the company of two dead men – one she adored, the other a devil right out of hell? Sweetie shook her head. *No,* she decided. She pulled her Pa's watch out from her skirt pocket and opened the lid to find it was only about 1:30 p.m.

She wanted to rise up and look out the window but first she needed to do a physical inventory. Her whole body ached from top to bottom but there were two, no, three areas that she knew needed attention. She reached up and winced at the cut on her lip. Edwardo had barged into her room and punched her so hard in the face she flew across the bed and hit the wall.

Her fingers danced lightly across her face, registering her painful and swollen nose, her cut lip and the bruises on her cheeks and neck. Then, hesitantly and with deep, abiding shame, Sweetie lifted her skirt and petticoat and saw the blood and other bodily fluids staining her crotch and upper thighs. Even as she gently probed the afflicted area, a freshet of new blood trickled through her fingers.

"Oh..." she muttered softly, as new tears dampened her cheeks. Thinking back, her memory was somewhat hazy and for that at least, she was grateful. She knew that Eddie Machete had come for her first as Billy drew back by the wall and watched with flat, emotionless eyes. She thought she'd been partially unconscious when the huge Mexican threw her on the bed, and didn't think anyone else took part in her rape, but to her mortification, she couldn't quite remember if Eddie was her only attacker or if he was just one of many.

Thinking that Billy, with his blank, deadened eyes had touched her, or Pete's pa might have taken a turn at her, was enough to make her stomach heave, and indeed, for a moment Sweetie thought she would vomit all over her own skirt.

Then, she pulled herself together and resolved to not think about it at all. At least until she got the hell out of here. Gritting her teeth, Sweetie grasped the side of her bed and hauled herself to her feet. She groaned as her injuries complained – her head pounded, and her bottom felt torn in half.

Then, she was standing upright and gazing out the window at the season's first snowfall. The flakes were as big and intricate as one of her Ma's lace doilies, and Sweetie knew that this precursor to winter would not last long.

She turned around and studied the two bodies sharing the room with her. Biting her lip and feeling waves of pain coursing through her body like a river current, she knew that she did not have the strength or energy to move, much less bury the bodies. Besides, the ground was cold and firm from the last few weeks of frosty weather.

She wanted to go – NOW! She could not be sure if the gang planned to make its way back here, or if that sheriff and his deputies would show first. Either way, she wanted no part of it. Not knowing what else to do, Sweetie pulled a slightly blood-stained quilt off her bed and covered her Pa's body. Then, she took a handful of dried autumn leaves that decorated her bureau and placed the foliage on Dean's chest.

Finished, she turned to Eddie's body which was already beginning to bloat and draw flies. Glaring, Sweetie wouldn't have recognized herself if a mirror had been held up to her face. Her bright blue eyes blazed – not with fear, or shame or sorrow, but with wrath.

She caught a gleam of silver in the folds of her sheets and bent down to pick up one of her Pa's old knives. She studied it with narrowed eyes for a moment and then she screamed in rage and plunged the blade into the dead man's right ear.

Horrified at herself, she stared at what she'd done and then burst into hysterical giggles as the man let out a long, gassy fart. Sobering, she stepped back as the dead body seemed to grin, and then she turned to her chest of drawers and chifforobe. Grabbing her old satchel, Sweetie stuffed a few changes of clothes inside, grabbed her toothbrush, a few coins, a comb and a serviceable hat.

She realized that her chest was heaving with nerves, and she took a deep, calming breath. Then she knelt down, kissed her father's cheek and ran out the door. Pausing briefly, she ran into Dean's bedroom and rooted through his change purse but only found a little silver change and about eight dollars' worth of bills.

Stood to reason, she figured. Anything Dean had of value would have long been seized by the outlaws. She knew where there was more cash to be had, though...and prayed that the ground was not too hard with frost that she couldn't dig it up. Sweetie screwed her old hat down on her head, grabbed the satchel with her Pa's loose change and headed downstairs.

Stepping into the kitchen, she walked to the sink and pumped cold water into the basin, Then, she wiped the blood and snot from her face and gasping, tried to clean up her nether region. It was painful, like fire, but she persevered, until the cloth came away clean. Her face was messed up again from pained tears, but she figured a little saltwater wouldn't kill her. Besides, she was almost certain that tears were not done with her just yet.

Gritting her teeth, she packed some bread, cheese, and back-strap into the bag as well as two canteens of water. Then, she looked around at the only home she'd ever known and felt her heart turn to ice. Whatever fond memories she might have felt for the place were gone now – ruined by the evil that had come to visit.

Sweetie sniffed once and strode out the front door. She looked around to be sure she was alone and then ran to the corral where her elderly horse was nibbling at what was left of a bale of hay.

She whistled softly, and Bayberry lifted his head, nickering. Grabbing a small bucket of oats, Sweetie shook it and the gelding trotted over to where she stood. As the horse munched the treat, she saddled him and forced the bit into his mouth. She hadn't ridden the horse in a couple of months, and Bayberry shifted in protest but didn't crowhop or argue over-much.

Looking around, she wondered about the livestock – what little was left. There was one milk cow, eight hens and two roosters. They had once owned two sheep, but Eddie Machete had desired mutton, so those two animals had ended up on the dinner table. Finally, there were four pigs, but the sow had died a couple of months ago and the young piglets had begun to run wild.

Not knowing what else to do, Sweetie shrugged and opened the gates to the pastures. She hoped that the remaining livestock would find their way to a neighboring farm rather than succumbing to winter's icy grip.

Glancing up at the sky, Sweetie frowned. The snow had stopped for the moment, but instead of warming up, the temperature was dropping. She had thought to ride the fifty miles, or so, into Spokane Falls but now she thought it would be better if she caught a coach out of the Granville area. That town was only about fifteen miles away and she thought that coaches into the bigger city ran once a day. Or so she hoped.

Meanwhile, she had one more stop to make along the way. Stepping up into the stirrups, Sweetie pointed her horse toward the woods and made her way to her favorite mushroom-picking spot, and the small fortune her Pa had hidden under an old, rotten tree trunk.

7

Just as Sheriff Race Hilton and his deputies made their cautious way toward the deserted house owned by Dean Mack, Sweetie walked her horse toward the mushroom patch. Unlike home, where the snow had melted before hitting the ground, this particular area was covered with snow at least four inches deep.

She reached down and gently touched the shovel she'd picked up at the last second on her way out. She was pretty sure she knew where the old log and her Pa's fortune was located but for a moment, she froze in confusion. Everything looked so different!

Then, she shook her head slightly and gently nudged Bayberry's ribs. He trotted forward and to the right about fifty feet, and Sweetie let out a gasp of relief. She could see the tip of that old log peeking out from the snow. It was noticeably familiar because it was riddled with old pecker holes.

Jumping down into the wet snow, she paused for a moment and looked around. All of her plans to flee would be over if someone saw her digging, but as far as she could tell, she was all alone. She knew she had to hurry, though. As she rode her horse up the mountain, she'd glanced down and seen a number of riders coming up the road toward her home. She had no way of knowing if it was a neighbor, the gang, or maybe that sheriff coming back. Either way, it was imperative that she grab the loot and ride away as quickly as possible.

She set to digging and sighed with relief that the ground was still diggable. It was rocky though and with every stroke of the shovel, snow showered over her. Within moments, she was covered with sweat and snow.

Dean had dug deep, and Sweetie was panting with effort by the time her shovel blade hit something other than soil. She grunted then and stood stock-still, paranoia seizing her mind and making her gaze dart here and there looking for hidden watchers. But, as before, she was alone.

She snorted and thought, *Alone – appropriate, I guess!* Sweetie let her heartbeat slow down and then sank to her knees and reached down into the cold, moist dirt. She was wearing gloves but still, she managed to break a fingernail off at the quick as she scrambled for her Ma's satchel.

Fingertips reaching blindly, she finally found a hard leather handle and pulled as hard as she could, but the bag wouldn't budge! Heart sinking, she couldn't imagine what the problem was, so she picked up the shovel again and using the blade as a rake managed to remove most of the dirt on top of the satchel.

Reaching into the hole, Sweetie grasped the handles and jerked them open so she could peer inside. Then, her mouth dropped open in shock. No wonder she couldn't just pull the bag out with ease – it was filled with gold. Bars, coin, bags of dust and a large leather envelope tied together at the top with stout metal staples.

Trembling, Sweetie pulled the bag out and used her teeth to pry the metal staples open. Then, she pulled a large swatch of papers out and started reading. Halfway through the first page, she hung her head and let tears of sorrow and relief fall from her eyes.

Her uncle Jed Cummings had, apparently, purchased a gold mine in California some years earlier and called it the LUCKY LADY. She didn't know the particulars, but the mine had struck big and Jed had come back home to share his good fortune with his sister and her family.

Jedediah had, apparently, cashed out on most of the mine's profits but there was something about residuals, and interest...the rest was too complicated to understand without help, and tears blurred her vision.

Taking a deep breath, she studied further and saw toward the end where Jed had willed his entire fortune to her, with her father acting as steward of the fortune until she turned twenty-one-years-old.

There was an additional envelope and Sweetie saw her Pa's scratching on it. Hands shaking suddenly, she opened the letter to see that he had willed any interest in the Lucky Lady mine to her. So, even though Dean's actions had spelled an end to her family, he was wise enough to know the peril he had put his brother and niece in and had taken steps to keep her future intact.

Sweetie's heart squeezed with sorrow and pity. Her uncle had come back with his fortune to find his sister dead, his brother-in-law embroiled with a gang of outlaws, his niece destitute of love and safety...and ultimately his own sorry end at hands of Dean's friends – turned enemies.

Dean had known of Jed's fortune and had tried, she knew, to throw off Billy's shackles but he was too weak to really rise up against the gang. Now, the gang was gone, her father and uncle dead, and she was left alone in the world.

Her tears dried up and suddenly, her body trembled with wordless rage. She was mad at her ma for dying and leaving her weak-willed husband rudderless and devoid of a moral compass. She was angry at Billy Drake for his keen insight into other men's weaknesses and his passionless ability to strike at the very heart of his enemies.

She was mad at her uncle for his innocent kindness and furious at Edwardo Martinez for rendering her helpless and grieving.

As she stared down at the large satchel of gold in the ground at her feet, Sweetie Mack swore that she would never, *EVER* be weak again. She would take this gold and make a new life for herself. A life where she held all the cards, and no man would cause her to stumble and fall, *ever* again.

And, if it was the last thing she ever did, she would hunt Billy Drake down like the damn, dirty dog he was.

8

Sheriff Race Hilton gazed down at Dean Mack and studied the faded autumn leaves someone had placed on his chest. *A wife maybe, or a daughter,* he thought. The room he and his deputies stood in was decidedly feminine.

One of his men, an oldster by the name of Clancy Delaney, spoke up from the far side of the room. "Her name is Sweetie Mack. Sounds pretty young from the writing in this diary."

Turning toward Clancy, the sheriff said, "Let me have a look."

Clancy stepped around the dead man on the bed with a look of disgust. The filthy-looking Mexican was deader than a doornail, but even now his body was exiting life by passing gas and grimacing fiercely.

The other reason for the deputy's sneer of dismay was the fact that the dead man's penis was still slightly engorged. Judging by the small drops of blood on the bottom sheet, which were separate from the blood on the coverlet, it was clear to every man in the room what the bandit had been doing before he was killed. In addition to the knife sunk deep into his ear, there were numerous stab marks on the man's neck and back.

Putting two and two together, Hilton figured the man was busy raping Dean Mack's daughter even as Dean had tried like hell to divert the sheriff's attention away from the house. Perhaps, once he'd stepped back inside the house, Dean had jumped on the man's back and stabbed his daughter's rapist until he himself was shot in the head.

What a pity, Hilton thought with a sigh, and looked down at the little diary in his hands. Going back a few pages, he saw a wealth of information about the bad gang of outlaws he and his men were currently chasing.

Hilton smiled slightly and tucked the book into his coat pocket. He would read it later, after he got this mess sorted out. Looking up, he saw one of his other deputies, a youngster named Terrence Booker, going through the few clothes in the chifforobe. "This is a girl's closet," he said, "but where did she go?"

Hilton's heart sank. Chances were good that the girl was either already dead or in the outlaw's clutches – they would not want her alive to stand witness to their crimes. *If only Dean Mack had said something to me,* he thought, *I might have been able to help!* But then he remembered the gleam of gunmetal in the upstairs window earlier this morning, the sense of many eyes watching his every move and his own haste in fleeing as quickly as possible.

Shaking his head, he said, "Well, there ain't much we can do for these folks now. Let's load Mister Mack up on one of the spare horses. Least we can do is take him into town for a proper burial."

He heard a chorus of agreement and the two younger deputies threw a blanket over Dean's body and prepared to carry him downstairs. They filed out of the house and into the yard.

"Look sharp, boys, you never know if those outlaws circled back..." the sheriff warned.

They paused on the porch and looking around saw nothing but a lone rider coming down a steep incline toward the house. The deputies dropped Dean's body gently on the porch boards and pulled their rifles. So did Clancy, but the sheriff murmured, "Hold steady, boys. I think that's a girl riding our way."

Sure enough, the men saw a slight, feminine figure walking her horse in their direction. Confirming her intentions, they also watched as she looped her reins around the saddle horn and held her hands up in the air.

"I think that's Sweetie Mack, sir," Terrence said.

Hilton agreed. "Go easy, but keep your guard up, okay? I want to make sure this is who we think she is, and not some female the gang uses as a decoy."

"Yes sir," they muttered.

***

Sweetie had spent a lot of time loading the gold into her saddlebags and trying to muffle any noise the metal might make as she traveled by wrapping her clothes around the bars and coins. She wanted nothing more than to take her new-found wealth and disappear but had reluctantly realized she needed help. She was simply too young, inexperienced and ignorant to hold onto what she possessed without some support.

Sweetie knew almost no one and had no idea who to trust, but she figured a "Lawman" would be a good start. For all she knew, the sheriff who had come by the house was as crooked as an old stick. But she also knew she had no chance of holding onto her inheritance unless she could prove that Dean Mack was her father, and she was the rightful heir to her uncle's fortune.

Just in case, though, she'd tucked a number of heavy gold coins in the band around her chest. She didn't think that a badge-wearing man of the law would remove her clothes to check her facts, but she couldn't be too careful.

Now, as she rode toward the men standing on her porch, Sweetie's heart started pounding in fear. They all looked like thugs – heavily armed, their faces shrouded in shadow. But as she rode slowly forward, a smaller man, wearing a big silver star on his coat, stepped out from behind another grizzled, gray-haired fellow and said, "Hello! My name's Sheriff Hilton, out of Spokane Falls, and these are my deputies. Are you Sweetie Mack?"

Sweetie's face turned white and she thought about turning her horse around and fleeing. Then, curiosity got the better of her and she asked, "How'd you know that?"

Hilton studied the young girl's face and his heart felt sore. Her long brown hair was tousled, and he could see that her nose was swollen, and her lip was cut. Her neck also seemed to be bruised and she was covered in mud. Her eyes were hollow as she stuck her chin out with a semblance of pride.

Turning to his men, Hilton murmured, "Put your weapons down, men. This is Sweetie, I'm sure of it."

His three deputies lowered their rifles and removed their hats in respect. As Sweetie watched them her bright blue eyes filled with tears. Swallowing her heart – which seemed to have crawled up into her throat – she asked again, "Do I know you?"

Sheriff Hilton shook his head and said, "No, miss, I don't reckon you do, but we found your diary. Is this here your pa?" He gestured to a quilt-covered shape on the porch, and tears fell in earnest from Sweetie's eyes, which she wiped away in frustration.

She nodded. "Yes, sir, if he is the one with a bullet in his forehead. The other one...that was Eddie Machete, uh, Edwardo Martinez. My daddy killed him right before Billy shot him dead."

The sheriff frowned. "Billy who?"

The girl looked confused. "Uh, I don't remember his last name, sir. But he was the one in charge."

"Okay, then," the sheriff sighed. Gazing back up at the girl he asked, "Are you okay, honey?" He knew she was far from okay, but she seemed to be a prideful little thing and he didn't want to embarrass her any further than she already was.

Sweetie nodded. "Yes. I'll be fine. I just, I just need a little help with my pa. Can you help me?"

"You bet. Me and the boys are riding back to Granville. We were fixing to take yer Pa to the sheriff's office there. I'm sure that Sheriff Matthew Wilcox will send for the undertaker if that's alright with you?"

Sweetie nodded and swayed suddenly in her saddle. The events of the day had caught up with her and now all she wanted to do was sleep, but she knew she had to stay with these fellers – at least for a while, until she was strong enough to head out on her own.

This little sheriff seemed to be a good man. Hopefully the Granville sheriff, Matthew Wilcox, would turn out to be a good man as well.

9

Two hours later, Sweetie and Hilton's posse rode into the little town of Granville. It had fallen into dusk an hour earlier and the two younger deputies had lit lanterns which hung from long, thin sticks placed into their rifle scabbards. The shadows they cast were eerie and mesmerizing.

Sweetie gazed at the dim, uncertain light and tried not to think about what her life had become. Her future seemed as eerie and uncertain as the lantern light, and she felt herself tremble with nervous anxiety.

Still, she thought, these fellows seemed nice enough and she knew she had been lucky. Sweetie spoke for the first time in three hours. "How soon before we get there?"

Sheriff Hilton turned in his saddle. "We should be there soon, very soon." He peered ahead and exclaimed, "There! That's the town stables and smithy – see the flames?"

Sweetie stared into the gloom and grinned. "Yeah, I see it. I only ever been here twice before, and it was daylight then." She had been worried about this new sheriff and what would become of her once Hilton and his men left. She expressed her thoughts now. "Sheriff, is Mister Wilcox a nice man?"

Hilton replied, "Oh, yes. He's one of the best lawmen in the county. I asked him and his crew if they wanted to head out with us today, but he has his own fish to fry, and really, most of the crimes committed by Billy Drake and his gang are taking place in the Spokane Falls area. We are Spokane Falls lawmen and the task falls to us to take those skunks down."

Sweetie didn't care if Wilcox was the best lawman in the world. What she really wanted to know was if he had a good heart, and if she could count on his decency to help her on her way to freedom- or not.

She said, "I guess I want to know if he's a nice man, like you."

Hilton grinned. "Yes, honey. He's as nice as can be and will do his best to help you. Hey, there's his deputy now – come to see who's riding in after dark. Hey, Roy, thanks for keeping the lanterns lit for us."

Sweetie saw a middle-aged man with short reddish-brown hair, standing just outside the stable fencing, holding a lit lantern aloft. "Hey there, Sheriff Hilton. Did you find your outlaws?" he asked.

Hilton shook his head, "We were close, but nah, they skedaddled afore we had the chance to nab 'em. We did a find a young lady who needs our assistance, though. Is the sheriff around?"

The deputy shifted his attention to Sweetie and his sad,

solemn gaze made the girl squirm. In answer to Hilton's query, Smithers said, "Yessir. He's down at the shed, doing paperwork." The deputy had done his share of paperwork for the Spokane Falls sheriff's department and was glad he no longer needed to toil in that regard.

"Yes," Hilton replied with a grin. "That's the bane of lawmen everywhere. Me, I'd rather be in a shoot-out with some bad gang than have to sit over county paperwork every dang night!"

"Yessir, me too." Roy grinned. "Why don't you head on down there and relieve Matthew of his duties. He will thank you for it."

Hilton smiled and said, "Well, we'll be off then. Have a good evening, Roy."

They moved forward down the street, and Sweetie saw that Granville was smaller than she'd remembered. She had only been to visit two times, and one of those times she was just a baby in swaddling clothes. The other time was a couple of years earlier, when the family had come to town for supplies and to see a traveling circus. Sweetie realized now that the town's population had been inflated then because of the festivities.

There was a small main street which included a general store, a post/telegraph office, a cafe, a bakery, a couple of bars, a hotel and a bath house/laundry. There were a few other businesses, but they were shut down for the night. Further down the street, she could see a few nice-looking houses.

Many of the homes' windows were lit up with lantern

and candlelight. It seemed to her that those houses were lit up with family and love. Intellectually, Sweetie knew that her own home had once been filled with the golden light of love, but since the gang came, darkness had descended and home had become a place filled with shadow, and fear.

Shrugging off her memories, she fumbled in her skirt and peered at her Pa's watch. *Yup,* she noted, *it is 7:45 pm.* Which was why the saloon and cafes were still doing a brisk business. As she looked around at folks walking on the sidewalk and stopping to converse, her heart ached.

Ever since her ma died, Sweetie had felt that the whole world revolved around her house, kitchen, barnyard and the tiny taste of freedom she experienced occasionally at the old mushroom patch. Now, seeing these gay folks visiting and hearing the tinkle of comradery and laughter, she realized that her existence had been reduced to that of a prisoner in a jail cell.

Sorrow threatened, yet again, but she savagely swallowed the emotions back down in her chest where they were safe and hidden – like the gold coins she'd spirited away from prying eyes.

They traveled another hundred feet or so, and rode to the right where a sign read, Granville Sheriff's Office and Jail. For a moment, her thoughts turned dark with suspicion. Could her rescuers actually be robbers, after all? Had they brought her here to place her in jail for the murder of her father and the bandit, Eddie Machete? Were they going to rob her of her gold?

Her thoughts spun like moths in the candlelight and then she remembered that technically, Hilton and his men knew nothing about the fortune she was sitting on, and they'd already confirmed that her pa had been killed by Billy's gang members. She cautioned herself to stay calm and not look a gift-horse in the mouth!

Heart pounding, she glared about and tightened her grip on Bayberry's reins. Then, she saw a door open on a little lean-to shed attached to the sheriff's office. A tall, slender man stepped out onto the boardwalk and tipped his hat to Sheriff Hilton, who smiled in return and said, "Howdy, Matthew. Brought you a visitor!"

Matthew Wilcox stared at the frightened young girl sitting her horse next to Sheriff Hilton. Both lanterns were lit outside the office and he could plainly see her bruised face and cut lip. The haunted look in her eyes was not lost on him either and he winced with sympathy. He knew an abused child when he saw one, and he vowed to help her if he could.

Stepping down off the boardwalk, Matthew walked to the girl's horse, and stuck out his hand to shake. "Hello, my name is Matthew Wilcox. I'm the sheriff around here. What's your name?"

Sweetie stared down at the man's handsome face and felt her heart begin to thaw. She reached down to shake the man's hand and said, "My name's Sweetie Mack. My pa... he died and now I need some help. Can you help me out, please?"

10

Things seemed to speed up then – faster than Sweetie was comfortable with. Another huge deputy named Abner Smalley came and led Bayberry behind the jailhouse where there was, apparently, a small barn and stable. Sweetie watched her fortune walk away and wanted to scream. However, she understood that she needed to stay calm and not let on that the saddlebags were filled with gold.

Then, she found herself inside the little side building next to the jail. It was warm inside and comfy with a cook-stove toward the back sending out waves of heat and the smell of good soup. Matthew invited her to sit on a small divan while he and Sheriff Hilton sat and discussed the particulars of the gang and her part in it.

She drank a cup of bitter coffee and relished a bowl of soup from the back of the stove while a giant wolf gazed at her from behind Sheriff Wilcox's desk.

Its golden-eyed gaze seemed to be filled with wisdom and tenderness. Afraid, at first, Sweetie set her bowl on the floor and whispered to the wolf to come and eat. Sensing his pet's interest, Matthew looked at the bowl on the floor and with a nod, signaled to the creature his permission to lick the bowl clean.

Immediately, the wolf came to the bowl, gave it a few cursory licks and then placed its large gray and black head on the couch arm. Sweetie smiled in wonder and stroked the animal between the ears until it got up and padded back to its master's side.

Then, as if the food was a drug, all the anxiety, fear and pain in her body went numb and she fell asleep. A small part of her urged caution but the weariness was overwhelming and she dozed as Matthew and Race talked.

Noticing, Matthew stood up and went to a tall bureau, where he fetched an old quilt and draped it over the girl's body. Turning to face the Spokane Falls sheriff, he said, "She's finally asleep. Now, we can talk."

Hilton nodded, and sighed with fatigue. He had sent his deputies down to one of the local cafés for supper and he hoped there was a room for let at the hotel. The day's ugly events were catching up to him, and shaking his head, he said, "I think that girl was used hard, Matthew. She hasn't said a word about it but me and my boys saw the evidence with our own eyes. We're guessing that the gang moved in on her and her pa some time ago – probably about spring-time. God knows what she's been through while they took over. I'm hoping she can tell us more, but first she needs to heal and get some rest."

Matthew frowned. Doc Dearbourne had come to fetch Dean Mack's body, and arrange for a proper burial, but had put some balm on Sweetie's cut lip and suggested she be brought into his office the next day for a check-up.

A tough question needed asking. "Do you think Sweetie's pa was a part of the gang?"

Hilton shrugged. "Hard to tell, he might have been, but most reports state that there are usually five members of the gang taking part in the crimes. Dean Mack would have been number six. I think I would have heard if there were more men than that." He paused to light up a stogie. "I'm guessing this Billy character just used the man's farm and livestock as backup. Either way, I hope you will bury Mister Mack in your fine new graveyard, for the girl's sake."

Matthew looked shocked. "Of course, I will…" Just then, Abner stepped inside and said, "Boss, there's something you oughta see." Matthew gazed up at the big man who added, "It's out back."

"Okay," Matthew answered, and turning to Hilton said, "Sheriff, you might want to see this too. Abner, stay here with the girl, okay?"

"Sure thing, Matthew," the deputy replied.

They stepped through the back door and walked about thirty feet to the Sheriff's stables. Bean Tolson, Matthew's third deputy, was rubbing down Sweetie's old gelding and her saddle bags were lying a few feet away against the back of the stall. "Over there, sir. I never would have opened them bags, but they were so heavy the weight about crippled this old horse." He bobbed his chin at the open bags.

Walking over and gazing down at the open saddle-gear, Matthew's mouth dropped open and sheriff Hilton whistled. "Hoo-eee!" he breathed, and Matthew agreed. Both bags were stuffed with gold- bars, coins and dust.

The same thought occurred to both men at the same moment. Was this gold part of the loot Billy's gang had been hoisting the last couple of years? If so, Sweetie's new-found fortune was forfeit and Matthew couldn't help but grieve for the girl.

She had a real chance at a life with this money, but the courts – although slow as molasses most of the time, were also inexorable in their pursuit of what they considered to be *their* lost money.

They heard a ruckus behind them and then a small, feminine voice said, "That's my uncle's money, sirs. I got the paperwork here to prove it. Also, the deed that says it's all mine."

Both sheriffs turned around and Matthew said, "Tom Tolson here, took the bags off your horse and noticed the weight. He didn't mean to pry."

Sweetie shook her head. "I know, and I'm sorry for it. Bayberry's a good old horse and I didn't mean to weigh him down so much, but I didn't know what else to do." The girl fumbled under her shirt for a moment and pulled out a large, leather envelope. Holding it out, she said, "Here, read these papers, okay?"

Seeing that Sweetie was still reeling with fatigue, Matthew said, "Sure, but let's go back inside where it's warm."

Nodding, Sweetie stepped past Abner and went back inside. Looking at one another, Matthew and Race bent down, picked the saddlebags up and staggered inside with the heavy load. Placing the double bags back by the far wall, they joined Sweetie by the desk.

She had placed the leather envelope on the desk blotter and now Sweetie sat and watched as first, Race Hilton read the pages and then, Matthew had his turn. She wondered as she watched the men's expressions whether she had just lost her inheritance because she'd been stupid enough to fall asleep at such a critical time.

However, both Matthew and Sheriff Hilton were starting to smile. Looking over at her, Hilton said, "Well, this is very good news for you, honey, and I, for one, am happy as heck for you."

Turning her gaze to the younger sheriff, Sweetie saw the man's green eyes gleam. "Here's what I propose, Miss Mack. In two days, I expect the circuit judge to make an appearance. He'll look over these papers and I'm sure they'll find them in order. I wish my Uncle Jon..." he paused, and the older sheriff shifted in his seat.

Sweetie didn't know what had made Sheriff Wilcox falter with emotion, but he recovered quickly and said, "Never mind. I've been reading the law, and I believe these documents are sound. Meanwhile, I've sent one of my deputies to fetch my wife, Iris. I expect her to arrive soon, and I want you to head home with her when she arrives. Is that alright with you?"

Sweetie nodded and sighed with relief. All she really wanted to do was take a long, hot bath and sleep for a week. She wished she could do it right here, but she knew that she was still terribly vulnerable and too weary to stay on her game.

Yawning, Sweetie smiled and said, "Thank you, sir. I'd like to meet your…" Then, as if a heavy blanket had fallen over her, she closed her eyes mid-sentence and fell into a deep slumber.

✱✱

Nine days later the girl was gone – disappeared from Matthew's ranch without a word of goodbye – just two heavy pieces of gold and the words, 'Thanks for yore kindness', scrawled on a piece of paper left on the dining room table.

That same day, Matthew's wife, Iris moved around the bed where Sweetie had rested. She bit her lip in frustration. *That little girl should have stayed here with us! We would have raised her as our own,* she thought.

Still, Iris was not surprised. Even though Matthew had managed, with Judge Henley's help to legitimize Sweetie's inheritance and transfer the actual gold bars, coin and dust into bank notes, the girl was as skittish as a wild horse, wall-eyed and easily spooked.

And who could blame her? Iris thought. Once she had ridden the cart to Matthew's little shed that night and saw the poor mite dead asleep on the divan; her face and neck bruised, her lips torn, Iris knew what had happened even before Matthew filled her in. And seeing the girl wince as she stood up from Matthew's couch, Iris knew that Sweetie needed the kind of help only a woman could give.

Which she had endeavored to do...but it wasn't enough. Iris' son and daughter, Abby and Sam, had done their best to make the girl feel welcome and, of course, the littlest one; three-year-old Chance, who could charm the birds right out of the trees, had adopted Sweetie as a new older sister.

For a moment, Iris had thought that Chance would turn the tumultuous tide in Sweetie's heart. The girl had stared, bemused and smiling, as Chance grabbed her hand and led her out into the backyard to see his pollywog collection and show her the rabbit hutch and the nest of tiny bunnies that had appeared a couple of weeks earlier.

Then, Sweetie had allowed herself to be hauled around the farm by Iris and Matthew's son, and was charmed by the boy's ready smile and sweet kisses. But, apparently, that wasn't enough to calm the girl's fears. Iris had lost count of the times Sweetie had whispered, "I gotta go, Ma'am, sorry, but I best be on my way..."

Iris stared down at the rumpled sheets in her arms and felt tears moisten her eyes. "She's too young to be on her own," she whispered, "way too young!"

Just then, she heard her husband say, "Iris, you can't save every wild critter that comes your way. You just can't."

Iris looked up and saw Matthew leaning against the door jamb. Dashing an errant tear from her eye, Iris nodded. "Oh, I know it, Matty. I do! It's just that the girl is rich, which means every Tom, Dick and Harry will be after her fortune. Not to mention, there's plenty of men who would just plain kill her for it. You know that better than I do!"

Matthew nodded. He was frustrated too. He'd asked around and found out that Sweetie had left on the 5:00 a.m. stage to Seattle driven by the father and son team; Davey and Thadius Dillon. Both good men and honest as the day was long.

There was technically nothing wrong with a young girl traveling on her own, and Matthew knew that Sweetie had been lucky. Both Davey and his boy Tad would see to it she arrived in Seattle safely. What became of her after they dropped her off was another thing entirely, but at this point, it was really none of his or his wife's business.

Making Sweetie stay against her will was nothing short of kidnapping and both he and his wife knew it. Still, Iris' concern was justified. He walked up to his red-haired beauty and took her in his arms. "You know," he murmured. "I have a feeling that girl will not let on that she has any money. She's as quiet as a church mouse. Still, just to be sure, I sent a wire to young Steven Mercer as soon as I found out that Sweetie had left.

"Oh!" Iris smiled. "That's that nice young district attorney you met last year, right?"

Matthew nodded. "Yes. I told him not to harass the girl if he can help it, but just keep an eye out for her. She's free to do what she wants to do with her life moving forward, but at least Steve will be close-by if he sees her being threat-ened. Of course, that will only last as long as she stays in the Seattle area, but it's the best we can do for Sweetie now."

"You are a good man, Mattie. Thank you." Iris mur-mured as Matthew folded her in his arms.

PART TWO

1905

PART I

11

Sweetie stretched her arms and grimaced with pain. Trask had worked her hard today, and although a heavy work-out was what she wanted, she couldn't help but feel that the old man had enjoyed himself entirely too much as he whacked her over and over again with his wooden practice sword.

Frowning, Sweetie wondered if she would *ever* learn to master her fencing rapier. Thinking (arrogantly) that she already had mastered the finer points of swordplay, she was put in her place this morning as her instructor grinned with glee and all the other men she had hired over the years shuffled their feet nervously, and murmured, "Come on, Trask, she's had enough" or, "Give her a break, man".

She had lost her temper then, and glaring, said, "Don't you men have something better to do than sit around watching me?" Now, Sweetie blushed just thinking about it. These men loved her and would do anything, she knew, to keep her safe. Sure, they were paid well to do protect her and her interests, but their affection toward her was genuine, and she had no call to berate them for their concern.

Deciding, abruptly, to treat them all to a fine dinner later on this evening, she laid back in the bubbles of her bath and lifted her right leg out of the water. She studied the dull purple and black bruises on her knee and lower thigh. That came from failing to pirouette while counter thrusting – a lesson she had been taught over a year ago but had, apparently, forgotten this morning. She rolled her eyes in disgust. Trask was right to give her a painful reminder as she herself had insisted on learning the skills of warfare – swordplay, gunfighting, hand-to-hand combat and knife-work.

To accomplish her goals, she would need to be just as tough, if not tougher than the men she aimed to take down! Sweetie closed her eyes and allowed herself to recollect the past seventeen years. She remembered perfectly well what had happened to her the day her pa died. Although she rarely dwelled on the more...personal aspects of Eddie's attack on her person, she knew that the rape had helped shape her current disposition.

What she did give full unyielding attention to, however, was what those men had done to her pa, and her uncle. Now that she was older, she understood that Billy Drake had not only stolen Dean Mack's house and home, he had also robbed her pa of his heart and soul. Sweetie shook her head now at how neatly the man had seized control of Dean's life – using his daughter's weakness and vulnerability against him and her uncle Jed's love for both of them to weave his deadly web even tighter.

Disturbed anew at her memories, she hissed and rose up out of the bathwater. Stepping out of the tub onto a bath towel, she strode to the full-length mirror and studied her reflection. Biting her lip, Sweetie felt both proud and annoyed at her own image.

She had grown tall- almost 5'10 inches which was freakishly tall for a woman at that time, and her body was honed to a fine edge. Looking past the numerous bruises, she studied her long arms which were thin but ropey with muscles, and at her belly which was flat and toned. Her thighs were sleek and her buttocks firm and strong. Her breasts were rather small, but she nodded in satisfaction. For her purposes, they were the perfect size.

Her face was, again, a mixed blessing. She had grown to be...pretty, and she didn't like it a bit. Any chubbiness in her face and cheeks had disappeared over the last five years of heavy training, leaving her with a bony, and raw-looking visage which was far from feminine. But...

Her eyes, as always, were the brightest of blue and her lips were finely etched and enticingly plump. Her hair was a rich chestnut in color and fell in waves to her lower back. Sweetie gazed down at a pair of scissors on top of the vanity. "Hmmm," she sighed, and sat down at the table to apply cream, and a powerful ointment to her to her many cuts and bruises.

She picked up her Pa's old pocket watch and studied the time. 8:40 am- plenty of time to do the many final preparations needed before she and her team left for Washington State.

Pouring herself a fresh cup of coffee, she thought about what had brought her to this place and time...

Sweetie would never forget the kind young sheriff, Matthew Wilcox in Granville, Washington and his beautiful wife Iris, and how hard they had tried to make her feel safe and welcome in their boisterous home. She remembered their little boy... Chance was his name, and his polliwog collection.

She recalled being sorely tempted to stay on there, but she also remembered how frightened she'd been of the gang who had wiped out her family and stolen her innocence. She had also felt that she was a magnet for foul creatures and bad luck, and worried that the sheriff's family could fall victim to that same misfortune if she lingered there too long.

That's why she'd finally left and made her way to the far-off city of Seattle. She grinned as she thought of Steven Mercer and his not-so-subtle attempts at protecting her fortune and her virtue. Apparently, Matthew Wilcox had set his friend to watch over her, and after demanding an answer, he had confessed it to be true. "It has been my pleasure, though," he added.

Sweetie grinned as she heard his voice, even now, calling out to one of the men in her employ; Randall Winters, who answered back in his soft Southern drawl. "It's been done and checked on twice, Steven. Stop worrying!"

Apparently, Steven was asking for something to be double-checked, and she smiled knowing that Steven was overly fussy and protective but was also held in high esteem by his peers.

Sweetie shook her head. Despite her precarious beginnings, she had been blessed by those who surrounded her now. Men she had hand-picked over the years to safeguard her and her fortune, and how she had reciprocated by helping to safeguard them in return.

She had spent about six months in the city of Seattle, while Steven clucked over her like a mother hen and then decided to go to California – both to secure the rest of her fortune and to gain an education and the training she would need to make her dreams come true.

She had thought to leave Steven behind, but he'd insisted on coming along. She remembered staring at him in bewilderment – *why would he want to do such a thing?* she'd wondered. She had already made it quite clear that she would not accept any untoward advances from him, and when she quizzed him about his motives, he'd merely shrugged and said, "I was tasked with looking out for you, and I figure letting you run off to Californy alone is hardly doing my job."

Sweetie remembered saying, "Well, I'm letting you off the hook now!"

But Steven had just shrugged and said, "That's not how it works, Sweetie. Besides, I'm tired of this place and would like a chance at a fresh start, if you'll allow me to accompany you." He had continued to study her face for a moment and then he added, "Sweetie, rest assured, I have no designs on your person, okay? For one thing, you're way too young for me and besides...you're just not my type. We'll look at this as simply a friendship – you watch my back and I'll watch yours. Can you live with that?"

Feeling a sense of relief that she didn't need to head off to an entirely new state all by herself, she's grinned and threw herself in Steven's arms. "Yes! We'll be partners, Steven. Maybe we'll get rich together, right?"

"Right," Steven had murmured and then hustled off to quit his job, gather up most of his belongings, store the rest, and purchase two train tickets to the land of gold and plenty. The train ride was long and boring but happily uneventful and a little over a week later they arrived in San Francisco.

It took no time at all to realize that his presence was absolutely necessary, and Sweetie, once again, blessed her lucky stars. She had gone down to the land offices (Steven in tow) and handed over her legal claim to residuals from the Lucky Lady gold mine and was informed, in no uncertain terms, that her papers were invalid, and her so-called residual earning were wholly the property of the new owners, Timothy and Jeffrey Barns. Sweetie also learned that although Jed had been told the claim was pretty-near played out, it was, in fact, one of the richest mines in the whole territory and pumping out gold and silver in astonishing amounts.

Immediately, Steven went to work. He had some money saved, but with Sweetie's financial backing, he was able to hang a shingle on the door of an upscale new law office, hire an excellent legal team, and sue the Barns and Co. mining outfit for lost income.

It took a while, and some political clout (Steven's father had once been the Attorney General of the new state of Washington and was good friends with California's governor) but eventually, the Barns brothers were forced to yield to the long arm of the law and pay Sweetie back a staggering $49,000 and change in lost revenue.

What was worse, at least to the Barns brothers, was the girl's demand that they rename the mine and let her keep the 'Lucky Lady' title for her own nefarious purposes. It was no big deal, really. They could name the mine after Satan himself, for all Sweetie cared, but there was something endearing about the title – something she wanted more than anything, for herself.

What she wanted was to be a lucky lady – not an orphaned and heart-broken shell of a girl but a woman to be reckoned with…a lucky lady who could and would avenge her family.

12

Sweetie reached for the eye shadow and powder on her vanity. As she dabbed the shadow on her eyelids and placed a small dot of rouge on each cheek, she let her thoughts walk down memory lane.

While Steven ran his thriving law office, she went to school. Mostly at home with an assortment of tutors, but she learned well and excelled in lessons that were quite unladylike...advanced math, the sciences, Latin and Earth sciences like Geology and Biology. She read and loved literature, and Steven coached her in the legal profession and what was and was *not* against the law.

She took cooking lessons and learned to knit and sew, run a large household and how to use elementary nursing skills and medicines. She hated these sorts of lessons but knew that she needed to be as accomplished as possible to gain her goals.

She also learned everything there was to know about horses, and sundry livestock. She bought a big new house in the western part of the city and filled it with paid servants. She even hired a lady-in-waiting to help her learn how to dress and comport herself in society.

Looking back, Sweetie realized that although it seemed like no time had passed at all, it had taken many, many years to become what she was today. A self-taught, desirable woman who was welcomed now into polite society, despite her uncertain past.

Investing wisely, she had also become one of the richest women in California, and one who was sought after vigorously by a number of eligible bachelors. She sighed. Not one of those men piqued her interest in the slightest – and as far as she could tell, the feelings were mutual – at almost 30-years-old, she was considered to be an 'Old Maid'.

Sweetie didn't mind, romantic love just didn't figure into the equation and probably never would. Billy Drake had stolen those tender feelings from her, along with her maidenhead, and she was too busy to feel the loss.

The last few years, with Steven's help, she had bought up real estate with a voracious appetite. She was now the proud owner of three restaurants, two saloons, and a high-end brothel (mainly because she identified with the women in that age-old profession and felt they had once been cast out of any normal life through circumstances entirely out of their control, just like she once was).

She also owned a half city block boasting Steven's law offices, a milliner's shop and a bakery. She collected rents on all of these businesses and could actually run most of the businesses on her own if needed.

Well, she mused, those businesses will be on their own, for a while. She was glad that she had hired Patrick Dover to run things while she was away. He was a kind and patient man, once a beat cop, who would collect rent without resorting to strong-arming and keep an eye out for the numerous crooks and villains who were always lurking about, trying to take from her all she had gained without putting in an ounce of work.

She sniffed, thinking, *let them try – Patrick will show them the error of their ways!* Still, she couldn't suppress the thrill of anxiety her final decisions had put into play. Her long-awaited plan was going into effect, starting tomorrow.

She frowned into the mirror and took a deep breath. *No! I will not turn into a nervous Nelly at the last moment.* Although her body was hard and keen, her heart had apparently gone soft with fear, and she gave herself a silent slap on the face.

Her spies had told her six months ago, about what had become of her old nemesis, and it was not to be tolerated! Billy Drake, who now called himself William Darcy, was living in high cotton in the Wenatchee area of Washington State. He was the mayor and lived in a luxurious mansion with a wife and two daughters. Although he had seemed ancient to her at the tender age of thirteen, he was only 50 years-old now, and he seemed to have the world on a string.

To make matters worse, he was surrounded by his old

gang members – all of whom had shed their wolf's clothing for worsted finery and served as his henchman in wrestling power from the citizens of Wenatchee and Chelan county!

Sweetie gulped and watched in the mirror as her cheeks flooded with rage. Kevin Woolsey, who she had once liked and looked up to, and the vile Peter Meadows were lawmen now and ran the city with iron fists. How these crooks had hood-winked the people of Chelan County and seized most of the towns and hamlets in the area with greasy fists was a mystery to her.

But that's all about to change, she thought. Taking a powder puff, she placed the cool, scented powder on her hot and angry cheeks.

***

About eight hours later Sweetie and her associates took seats at a table by the windows of the Cliff House Restaurant. Overlooking the Pacific Ocean, this was a premiere hotspot for the social elite. Sweetie and her friends cared nothing about that but the novelty of eating fresh clams, crab and lobster overlooking the bay in one of the toniest joints in town held their attention, plus the fact that their darling Sweetie was footing the bill for the treat.

She had approached them earlier that morning and apologized for snapping at them during her fencing lessons. They all knew she was taking a pounding, and figured they'd be snappish too but, as usual, Sweetie was trying to let them know that they were more than employees to her.

In her mind, they were her best friends in the whole world.

Every man there felt the same way about her. Only a couple of them really knew Sweetie's history – Steven and Edwin Trask. But all of them had been saved by her, in one way or the other.

Randall Winters had been plucked out of a California prison...his crime? Being a black man in a white man's world. Randall had been waiting for his horse to be shoed when a bank robbery occurred two hundred feet away from where he sat enjoying a bacon sandwich, and a mug of sweet tea.

He had no idea what was going on except for the fact there was a helluva hullabaloo down the street. Standing up to see what the ruckus was about, he was suddenly approached by two sheriff's deputies and told to get down on his knees and put his paws up!

Before he knew it, he was in handcuffs and sitting in jail – framed for the robbery and subsequent murder of two bank tellers. No amount of pleading his innocence helped him – in fact, no attorney would take his case at all. Except for Steven Mercer.

Somehow, the lawyer had gotten a hold of Randall's files and after studying the situation (apparently, two local college boys had gotten it into their heads to lift some cash from the small bank – rumor had it the stolen money was to be used to pay for a back-alley abortion for the girlfriend of one of the boys. The boy's fathers, one a city council member, and the other a well-to-do horse breeder had decided to pin the crime on the closest available Negro rather than see their boys hang).

Steven, ever the champion of the down-trodden, took the case to the California Supreme court...and won. Needless to say, Randall owed his life to Steven Mercer and to Mercer's young friend, Sweetie Mack. More than that, though, he loved both of them and would do anything to keep them safe and sound.

Edwin Trask was an old friend of Steven's father. A retired Army Colonel, he had thought about hiring on as a part-time sheriff's deputy, or a security guard somewhere, as he was still a vigorous man at 64-years-old, and lonely at home since his wife had gone on to her reward.

One phone call from Adam Mercer, however, sent him to the state of California, where he found himself employed as a security guard for a young lady named Sweetie Mack. He had never looked back and even now did whatever he could to watch the girl's back.

Her taste in food, though, is terrible! he thought as he stared quizzically at the bright red shell and small, beady eyes of a King crab on the table in front of him – which seemed to be staring right back at him with the same expression on its face!

Patrick Dover smirked at the look on Edwin's face. "Have you ever eaten a crab before, Ed?"

Trask shook his grizzled head. "Nah, don't like the look of them. Figured something that looks like a spider would probably taste like one too... stands to reason, anyway."

Dover grinned. "Well, in this you're wrong, sir. Me da and I used to go crabbin' and lobster'n all the time – made a pretty penny at it too, before he passed – God rest him." Spearing a large piece of lobster meat, he placed the tasty morsel on the Colonel's plate and said, "Now, dip that meat in some of this here butter, you'll like it, I promise you!"

Trask looked like he wanted to say NO! but after glancing at Sweetie's smiling face, he sighed, dipped the lobster meat in the melted butter and put it in his mouth. Suddenly, his expression transformed into a state of ecstasy and he smiled in pleasure as the rest of the party laughed at his surprise.

Sweetie studied the faces around her and felt a tingle of fear. From Patrick Dover, an Irish immigrant and fellow orphan, to the formidable Colonel Trask, she had been truly blessed to find such men. She frowned, though, even as her men laughed and teased each other at the fancy table with an ocean view.

She was about to ask too much of them – maybe all, and she hadn't the right. They were all safe now and comfortable. None of them needed to risk everything to fulfill her dreams of justice!

Oh, she knew that Patrick would be fine since he was simply staying home and managing her many business concerns, but the others! What right did she have to ask so much of them?

Sighing, she picked up her wine glass, and proposed a toast. She started by saying, "We'll be leaving on the train tomorrow morning at seven-thirty AM. First, I want to thank all of you for being the best friends anyone could ask for. Cheers!"

With smiles all around, the men lifted their glasses and murmured, "Cheers, Sweetie. Hup, Hup!"

Then, in a low voice Sweetie added, "And now, I want to give each and every one of you one more chance to step away from what is sure to be a hazardous, even deadly mission..."

13

Of course, every man in Sweetie's employ proved loyal and more than willing to go to Washington State to bring her enemies to account. They had worked for the young woman for years, cared for her, and couldn't imagine not trying to help her out now, when she needed them the most.

Two days later, everyone but Patrick Dover sat in a hotel suite in Seattle, going over final plans. Sweetie had spoken to Randall about what the bandits, Billy Drake and his men, had done to her and her family so long ago and what she intended to do about it now. He was in total agreement. He had often been the target of discrimination and injustice and wanted to stand by this young lady now.

"So, is it ready to open, Steven?" Sweetie asked.

Mercer nodded and smiled. "Yes, mostly. The bar is ready, but we're still waiting for the two industrial cook stoves for the kitchen to arrive from Chicago, which should be in about eight days. We also need to hire staff, but we're on schedule to open by month's end."

"And you still believe the saloon is located in a good area...an affluent area?" she wondered.

Steven nodded again. "I have never visited the Wenatchee area, Sweetie, but one of my oldest friends says the East side of town is quite the going concern. It's located along the Colombia River and there are many houses being built there, along with successful farms, orchards, grocers, and restaurants. There's a lot of commerce and, apparently, money there too, so a new saloon will be welcomed, I'm sure. Especially since the two other drinking establishments in the vicinity are run-down and seedy holes-in-the-wall that most respectable citizens try to avoid by heading into the city proper to eat and drink."

Sweetie nodded and smiled. A year earlier, she had authorized the purchase of two acres of land in East Wenatchee and hired builders to erect what was now being advertised as the LUCKY LADY SALOON. It was going to be a grand place – two-storied with a family-style restaurant in front and an elegant bar towards the back. The upstairs apartment would house the bar manager and his family (if he had one), and there were three offices – one for Steven, one for herself and one for the security staff. There were also two large storage rooms to store cases of alcohol in.

She had spared no expense – there were brass fitting and three large, electric chandeliers. The bar was solid oak and the large mirror behind said bar was of the highest quality. There was a long shelf toward the back of the bar that would be home to nightly appetizers, and five roomy booths with dark curtains for those who sought privacy in their affairs.

The restaurant would also be a fine place for any up-standing citizen to meet and bring their families to dine. Evidently, the chef Sweetie had hired was already on the job. His name was Curtis Guthrie, out of Los Angeles, and he was known throughout the state of California for serving the best home-style cooking with an elegant European flair.

He had been given carte-blanche and was, even now, ordering in the finest plate and silverware, curtains, artwork, linens and crystal glasses. He had also put a local florist on retainer to fill the table vases with fresh blooms every day the restaurant was open, which would be six days a week.

Sweetie had heard that anticipation of the new saloon was at a heightened pitch, and local citizens stopped by daily, gazing in excited wonder at the army of workmen who painted, installed glass windows and hung signs. "When's she gonna open?" they quizzed the workers, and hollered, "Who're the new owners – anybody local?" Only to be shrugged at and ignored.

She had read a newspaper that featured a grainy photograph of her new saloon. To her eyes, the place looked imposing and almost too elegant for such a humble place. Still, Steven assured her that many of the homes being built in the area were huge and of the finest quality, and the tax rolls were teeming with new money and old wealth.

Satisfied, she said, "Well, we'll leave in the morning, okay? Looks like there are still quite a few things that need doing before the grand opening and I want everything to go off without a hitch." Frowning, she asked, "Steven, have you found a good bartender yet?"

The older man answered, "I have a number of applications for bartenders, but I thought we'd do those interviews together. A good bartender can make the place but a bad one...well, I don't have to tell you."

Sweetie nodded and sighed. Yes, they had recently fired what they thought was a great barkeep, named David Tully, only to find that over the seven months he'd run one of Sweetie's bars, the man had lifted almost $3,000 in profits. His firing was a sad, sorry affair that neither one of them wanted to experience again anytime soon.

"Okay. I need to go shopping now – you know why – but please try not to act too surprised when you see me in the morning." She blushed.

Randall grinned, but Trask looked concerned. "Are you sure you still want to go through with this part of the scheme, honey?" Trask was older and set in his ways about the fairer set – he loved the female species but firmly believed the fairer sex was frail – weaker than their more masculine counterparts. In short, he was scared for her.

Sweetie grinned. "In many ways, my outlandish height will work to my advantage, for once. Try not to worry, Edwin, I'll do fine. And if I don't, I've always got you guys with me, right?"

The men agreed, but Trask had his doubts. Sweetie had somehow gotten it into her head that she was huge and masculine looking, but as far as he was concerned, she was all girl, and a beautiful one at that.

Swallowing his unease, he allowed a small smile to cross his lips as they all got up to attend to the last-minute details. *Just let them try to hurt my little girl,* he thought, *and they'll learn the error of their ways, right quick!*

***

Sweetie and her partners arrived in Wenatchee by train the next day at about 4:30 p.m. The spring air was balmy, and as they drove to the Lucky Lady Saloon, Sweetie could smell apple blossoms on the late afternoon breeze. She caught glimpses of the Columbia River, and she could see evidence of wealth all around her, in the many farms, new houses, and cobbled streets. There were even new-fangled streetlights installed on the avenues, and as they pulled up to her new establishment, one of those lights illuminated the LUCKY LADY SALOON.

Randall whistled, "Wow, Miss Sweetie. Your new place is a dandy!"

Steven and Trask also voiced their approval, and Sweetie couldn't help but feel a thrill of maternal pride. What had started as a dream had turned out to be a jewel of craftmanship, with shiny peach colored clapboards and burgundy trim. Two brass sconces lit up the solid oak front door and even now she could see that someone, probably Curtis, was inside bustling about.

She smiled fondly, then sighed with regret. *There it is... just hanging in plain sight like ripe fruit ready to be picked! Too bad it's all a sham,* she thought.

✳✳✳

Curtis caught movement from the corner of his eye and looked out the window at the approach of four well-dressed men and a fancy coach and four. Suddenly nervous, he realized that these men must be the owners of his fine new restaurant.

Glancing about, he hoped that he'd not been too over abundant in furnishing the place. He'd been told to purchase whatever he needed to make for a fine dining experience but gazing at the dozens of shipping crates filled with the finest plate, silverware and crystal vases, he felt embarrassed by his enthusiastic purchases. *Guess, I'm about to find out what the new bosses feel about my spending habits,* he thought with a gulp.

The men stepped up on the wide veranda and walked through the front door. Curtis stood in the middle of the room with a long length of silk drapery in his arms, and said, "Hello! May I help you?"

What an interesting group of men, he thought.

There were two older men – a venerable, gray-haired man with white chin whiskers and a military bearing, and a Negro gentleman in a fine, black suit. He was a thin man, with large brown eyes and a shy smile.

In addition, there were two younger men – one in his middle thirties with soft blond hair and a slight paunch, and another even younger gent with short brown hair, a slender build and large round spectacles on his angular face.

The blond man stuck out his hand to shake and said, "Hello. My name's Steven Mercer and this is my little brother, Martin. We're the owners of this establishment, and these men are our business partners, Edwin Trask and Randall Winters."

I knew it! Curtis thought and shook his bosses' hands. All four of the men were looking around with interest, and he stammered, "Hi! I'm the chef you hired, Curtis Guthrie. Sorry, the place isn't quite set-up yet, but it should be ready to go in a coupla weeks."

Steven smiled as his little brother walked to one of the boxes and pulled out a crystal brandy snifter. He turned it this way and that and ran a finger around the rim until a soft harmonic ringing filled the air.

Then, he carefully set the glass back in the packing straw and nodded with satisfaction. Steven grinned and said, "Looks like you have things well in hand, Mister Guthrie. Has the upstairs furniture arrived yet?"

Curtis nodded. "Yes sir, last week. Beds, bureaus, lamps, and some bedding. There are also two desks sitting up on the landing, but I left them where they were, because I wasn't sure where you want them placed."

"We'll take care of that, Curtis, don't worry. The only thing you need to worry about now is taking care of the kitchen, bringing in supplies and hiring your staff. I hear the stoves are still about a week out?"

I get to hire my own staff. He mused in relief. A good kitchen needed to run like a well-oiled machine and if he actually had control over who was hired, he could make this restaurant into something for the ages! He grinned at the new boss, and said, "I built a fire under those stove-makers, sir. They'll be here on Tuesday!"

He heard footsteps behind them and saw the three other men making their way upstairs. Turning back to the man in front of him, Curtis asked, "Can I bring you some coffee or tea, sir?"

Steven nodded. "Yes, thank you. We're here to stay now. Please, don't worry about our presence here, okay? We'll be in and out, making sure the restaurant and bar are ready for the grand opening. At least until the kitchen is operational. Don't worry about feeding us either…and, when we *do* eat here, consider us paying customers.

Oh, this place will be in the black from the get-go! Curtis silently crowed with delight and approval, but said, "Yes, sir," in a quiet, respectful tone of voice.

"Well then, carry on, Mister Guthrie, and well done!" Steven said with a smile before heading upstairs to meet with his brother and friends.

14

The next ten days flew by in a wink, as more equipment and people showed up to ready the kitchen and bar for business. Curtis, who required the largest staff, was busy morning, noon and night hiring additional cooks, dishwashers and wait staff. As far as Sweetie could tell, he was doing a good job.

His wait staff consisted of mainly older women, attractive but not beautiful, each of them swift, intelligent and clean. His kitchen staff was comprised of men, mainly, with one exception – an elderly Italian woman who was renowned for her baking skills.

Trask was in charge of hiring the bartenders and security team; those men who would monitor the saloon and help keep the riffraff out. He chose the Stine brothers- Scott and Ronald as bartenders. They had run a fair-sized saloon in downtown Wenatchee for almost a decade, until the whole place was shut down and seized by a private party.

Trask read the reports his private investigator had

compiled. This so-called private party was rumored to be none other than the mayor, William Darcy, along with his henchmen, Kevin Woolsey and Peter Meadows.

Trask's cheeks blushed with rage as he re-read the reports. This town was filled to the brim with crooks – the 'white-collar' kind of outlaw who hid behind a veneer of respectability and committed their crimes; graft, recontouring, extortion, bribery, blackmail, theft, even murder behind closed doors with a pen rather than a sword.

There was a pattern here – if a new business found itself happily in the black, the owners of that establishment soon found themselves ousted, whether they liked it or not. Most of these business owners didn't even try to fight. If they were smart, they limped away from their dreams with a small payoff in cash, although far less than what their businesses were actually worth.

But that was because the alternative was grim. Business owners who *did* try to fight, according to the private eye he'd hired, had found themselves and their families beaten – even killed – and their establishments burnt to the ground.

Trask glared. The intelligence they'd received in California was sound, and he worried about it daily and lost sleep at night thinking about the blatant corruption in the area, and the lengths these crooks were willing to go in achieving their goal...which was, apparently, owning Chelan County, lock, stock and barrel.

Where is the law? he wondered but added, *oh yeah, bought and paid for by the mayor himself!* Sweetie was right, her enemies were gathered here in Wenatchee, and they hadn't softened over the intervening years. If anything, they'd gotten worse!

The reason Trask worried now, though, was more personal. He had once been a formidable man, a revered Lt. Colonel, strong of mind and stout with muscle. Now, he was a shell of that man. Oh, he was still stronger than most men, and well-learned in the art of war, but he was slowing down. His muscles no longer responded to his every command, and arthritis bent his wrists and hands in unnatural and painful contortions.

He easily grew short of breath, as well. *Years of pipe smoking,* he mused. But he knew that in a fight, a man needed good lungs and a strong constitution to prevail and he was scared that if push came to shove in their upcoming battle against Sweetie's enemies, he might not be able to adequately defend his young charge.

Steven could shoot pretty well, but he was no fighter, and old Randy was just that...old and frail. He was good at what he did, and loyal to a fault, but what Trask needed now was muscle – and plenty of it!

He had already hired one young man by the name of Bradley Gooding. He was not terribly big, but he could shoot a treat and out-wrestle a snake. He was raised on a local farm and came highly recommended by many folks who'd seen the kid muscle bulls, horses and mules to ground for money.

What he needed now, though, was two or even three

big men – men who were loyal but mean at heart…the kind of mean that takes over when the stakes are high, and a faint heart led only to death and destruction.

Abruptly, Edwin decided to take the buggy downtown Wenatchee to the local boxing gym. He knew that the kind of men he needed liked to hang around in gyms, either for the feel of their muscles filling with the blood of battle rage, or simply looking for the extra cash offered in a scheduled prize fight.

He got up from his desk and wandered out into the hall, looking for Randall Winters. Walking by Sweetie's quarters, he saw her sitting on the bed and trying out new riding gloves. He knocked, and said, "Got a minute, Marty?"

She looked up and smiled. "Come in, Edwin. I'm just trying on some new gloves. Close the door, please."

Trask complied and looked at where Sweetie stood by her bureau with a sour look on her face. "Twice now, I've heard people talk about how soft my hands are. This has to stop, or I'll give myself away. I'm already practically standing on my tongue to keep from talking!"

Rumor had it that the younger Mercer brother must be a homosexual, because his skin was so fair and his voice so soft. Trask had been angry at Curtis, who'd overheard and reported the claim, but he stayed silent, for there was truth to it. Sweetie had an uncommonly low pitch to her voice – for a woman – but there was a fluty, breathless tone in her words that was too feminine to ignore.

It was the little things – her soft voice, fine complexion

and thin neck that give a lie to her acting job and made Trask sweat with anxiety.

Sweetie continued, "I don't mind being thought of as a sodomite – at least I won't have young ladies competing for my attention again!" Sweetie smirked, but Trask could sense her frustration. One of the waitress' younger sisters had taken a fancy to Martin Mercer and almost caused a scene when she was rebuffed.

Edwin knew that a woman scorned could be a big problem but somehow, Sweetie had managed to thwart the girl's desires without causing too much hurt in the process. Still, any threat right now could spell disaster to their plans and bring about a life or death situation.

Trask cleared his throat, and murmured, "I've said it before, and I'll say it again. Maybe you should head out of town while we do this sting? Go back to Seattle, or even Spokane..."

Sweetie shook her head, her eyes glinting in anger. "Mister Trask, if you please, I've already said that I'm not going anywhere. Perhaps, if you have so many doubts, you should head back to California? I'm sure Mister Dover could use your wise council!"

They glared at one another for a moment, and then Edwin smiled in defeat. "I'm sorry, lass. I've gone and done it again, haven't I?"

Sweetie's gaze softened. "And I'm sorry too, Edwin. Please forgive me. I'm just mad because I thought I'd be a better actress than I am. It's so frustrating!"

Trask grinned. "You're a fine actress, really. There are just some things a person can't hide...like being a woman in a man's world."

She nodded. "Yes, I'm figuring that out now. Oh well, with the grand opening in three days, I'm sure this tasty little saloon will draw the rats in droves. As soon as that happens, we can get our men and be on our way."

Trask agreed. "Yes, this place is drawing a *lot* of attention. I doubt if the mayor will show up right away, but his deputies will, for sure. Just...just promise me you won't let them see you, okay?"

Sweetie smiled. "I promise, Edwin. There is too much at stake to show my cards quite yet."

15

Once Trask found Winters they jumped in the buggy and headed toward the downtown area to a place called Gardner's Gymnasium. Sure enough, Trask saw a number of big, muscular men loitering inside, either waiting for their turns at the speed bag or warming up for a practice round in a dilapidated boxing ring.

The two men stood by the back wall and watched as one boxer after another made their way into the ring. Most of them were quite good, and Trask figured they were regular prize fighters in the employ of Jimmy Gardner himself.

Randall studied a flyer pinned up on a bulletin board and saw that a fight was scheduled for Friday night. **Tom THE BLACK CAT Kirwin vs. MIGHTY** Maxwell Cummings read the headline.

"Looks like we picked a good time for the grand opening," Randall murmured. "Big fights usually draw a crowd and we want that crowd at the Lucky Lady, not here."

"Right," Trask agreed. "Say, what'dya think about that

one?" He pointed at a huge man who was currently jabbing at the face and breastbone of his opponent in the ring. The man was being backed up, step by step, and was only inches from the rope. Once there, Trask knew he would have no place to go and the bigger man would prevail.

Winters looked at the winning fighter and saw determination in his face, but no cruelty. Even now, he was asking the smaller man if he wanted to concede defeat. The smaller guy shook his head, though, and with a shrug the big man clipped his foe's chin and he fell to the canvas in a heap.

Cheers filled the room, and Trask asked one of the bystanders, "Who is that fighter?"

The man received some cash from another fellow who had, apparently, lost a side bet and turned to Trask with a grin. "Why, that's the Black Cat, himself! I just know he's a gonna beat Mighty Max come Friday, and I can't wait to see it."

Trask nodded, said thanks and turned to Randall. "Let's go talk to the Black Cat, okay?"

"Sure thing, sir," Winters answered, and they made their way to the back of the gym. Tom (Black Cat) Kirwin was standing by a deep sink, splashing water on his face and chest. He was smiling at a joke one of his friends had just told and he didn't even look winded.

Trask thought he might have found his man, but he needed to do a little interviewing first. Stepping toward the fighter, Trask asked into the sudden silence, "Could we have a word with you, please?"

Trask saw the man stiffen. Then, without turning around he asked, "Who's asking?"

Hmmm. This man has seen trouble...maybe he's even in some trouble with the law? Or worse? Trask thought. "My name is Edwin Trask, and this is one of my partners, Randall Winters. We represent the Lucky Lady Saloon and we are looking for a couple of good bouncers for the bar. We just watched you fight and thought you could stand a steady job. Are you willing to talk to us?"

Tom hesitated for a moment and then he turned around to face them. All of his friends turned to face them as well. Tom looked to be in his middle thirties. He was a handsome cuss with jet-black hair, high cheekbones and deep brown eyes. Those eyes were not smiling now, however, "That place won't hardly last a week. Why would I give up my day job for a sinking ship?"

Trask glanced at Randall, who winked in return. *So,* Trask thought, *the corruption in the area is a well-known fact – not just rumor and speculation!*

Trask looked around and saw anger in many of the men's faces as they acknowledged the truth in Tom's words. He nodded and said, "Yes, we've heard there are a few rotten apples in this town." He heard some of the men snort at the word "few".

"That's why we want to hire two more men – to help enforce the peace and keep The Lucky Lady out of these crook's hands. Want to be a part of that?"

Tom frowned. "You know, the men you are talking

about flat stole my smithy from me. The same smithy that was handed down to me from my dad, and his dad before him. It was a good shop and turned a profit until Mayor Darcy and his men wrestled it from me."

He crossed his mighty arms and his face was kind but firm. "It's a losing game around here, fellas, and I don't know if I want to get mixed up with their kind again, now that I got a way to bring meat to the table for my family."

The men surrounding Tom were growing agitated and both Trask and Winters heard them echo Tom's words. They heard snippets of discussion like, "They stole my uncle's printing press, you know," and "They done killed old Barney when he wouldn't give up his wife's dress shop!"

Knowing he was taking a big gamble, Trask said, "Well, we aim to make some changes, gentlemen. All we need is a couple of good men to help us achieve our goal."

Turning to Winters, he said, "Did you bring cards with you, Randall?"

Winters smiled and reached into his vest pocket. Pulling out several business cards, he handed one to Tom Kirwin and a few more to the watching spectators. "Please, call us or feel free to stop by if you change your minds. Our grand opening will be next Saturday night. We could really use your help and the pay is good – very good!"

Trask smiled and tipped his hat. "We really hope you'll join our team, sirs. Have a good day."

Then, Trask and Winters took their leave.

***

Just as Trask and Winters made their way back home, Sweetie was trying to push her heart back down her throat to her chest where it belonged.

She had been outside supervising the landscaping in front of the saloon. Three young men, who were the grandsons of Nina Bartonelli, (the pastry chef) were helping her plant trees, shrubbery and grass seed. They had pretty much finished up and the boys had gathered together the rakes, shovels and general rubble from the front entrance and carted them around back to the garden shed, when a buggy approached.

She was covered in sweat and dirt from her labors and had just taken off her cap to wipe her forehead when she spied Kevin Woolsey pull to a stop in front of her saloon and take a long look around.

He had grown fat in his older years and hardly resembled the strapping young man she'd once known. But his sandy-blond hair was the same and he wore the same handle-bar mustache. He also wore a gawdy tin star on his jacket and sported an angry scowl.

She wanted to flee from his searching eyes but didn't want to make any sudden moves lest she catch his gaze. So, she settled for putting her big, round spectacles on and bending over to pick up a couple of pots the shrubbery had come in.

She hustled up the front steps, and heard Kevin shout,

"Hey you, boy! When's this place due to open?"

She didn't want to answer. After all, when she was younger, she had liked and trusted Kevin Woolsey and spoken to him quite freely. Years had passed, she knew, and odds were, he wouldn't recognize her voice now, but her heart clamored in her chest. If she turned around, and he remembered her face the game would be over!

Just then, Trask and Winters pulled up in the buggy and Sweetie flew inside with a gasp of fear.

16

Trask stepped out of the buggy after observing Sweetie fly through the front door, and approached the star-wearing man who was sitting his horse in front of the saloon. "Hello! Can I help you, sir?"

The man glared down at him and growled, "Who is the owner of this joint?"

Trask smiled, but his nerves tingled in alarm. "Well, this is a partnership of four. We are investors out of California. Why do you ask?"

Woolsey studied the front of the Lucky Lady, and answered, "I'm deputy sheriff Kevin Woolsey and I was sent here to see if your licenses are all in order." Gazing down at Randall Winters, a look of scorn crossed his face, and he asked, "What is your name, sir, and what's your boy's name?"

Trask's cheeks flushed with wrath. "My name is Edwin Trask, and this is one of my business partners, Randall Winters. We are *equal* partners," he added with emphasis.

"And, to answer your previous question, yes. The business licenses are all in order. You can run down to City Hall and see for yourself, if you like."

Meadow's eyes grew wide and his lips tuned down into a bitter grimace. Trask wasn't sure if it was because their licenses were in order, or the fact that Randall could actually be an equal partner in any business venture. After sitting silently for a moment, Woolsey spat, "Well, I'll be heading to City Hall directly. Those licenses better be legit, or your place won't be opening at all!"

Trask drew on all the dignity bestowed on him from a lifetime of illustrious service. Squaring his shoulders and glaring up at one of Sweetie's enemies with disdain, he said, "Do as you please, sir. You will find that the papers are filed and recorded. We'll be opening in three days' time, at any rate. I hope you'll join us. Until then, my *partner* and I are busy. Good day to you."

Then, both Trask and Winters turned their backs on the deputy, walked up onto the front veranda and stepped inside the saloon as Kevin Woolsey watched with narrow eyes.

✳✳✳

Trask and Winters found Sweetie upstairs cowering in her room. She dried her tears as the men entered and smiled. "Well, that's one of them, anyway. Now you won't need me to point him out."

Trask saw that the young woman was shaking with nerves and left-over fright. "How're you doing, Sweetie?"

She took a deep breath and replied, "I'm actually shocked at my reaction, fellas. So much time has passed, I didn't account for how I'd react when one of those...those bastards finally showed up!"

"It's understandable, Ma'am," Winters murmured. "Anyone would feel the same as you."

She smiled at the older man's concern but shook her head. "Maybe, but I can't. If I wanted to forget, I should never have come here. But now that I am here, I have to be strong, not fall apart at the first whiff of a skunk. Especially when Billy Drake makes an appearance."

"Consider this a practice run, okay? Even the finest soldier will suffer a case of nerves on the eve of battle. It's natural, Sweetie," Trask said.

Sweetie asked, "Well, what did you three talk about while I was up here with a case of the vapors?"

Trask grinned. "He wanted to know if we had the proper papers and licenses. I figured that would be the first thing Drake and his henchmen tried to pull, so it was the first thing I...I mean *we* took care of."

Winters added, "He didn't look too thrilled that a Negro could be a full partner in a business, either. I thought the Civil War might have helped with those kinds of feelings," he sighed.

Trask and Sweetie looked at the sorrow on his face, and although Sweetie didn't have the words to comfort him,

Trask said, "Some of my finest troops were men of color, Randall. Don't pay attention to bad men and their bad attitudes. Besides, the only thing we're really partners in is taking care of our girl, right?"

Winters nodded and smiled.

Suddenly there came a knock at the door. "Hello? Trask, are you in here?" They heard Steven's voice and Trask said, "Come in, Steven. We're just visiting with young Marty."

The door opened and Steven hustled inside. Seeing the dried tears on Sweetie's cheeks, he demanded, "What's wrong? What's happened?"

She held up her hands. "Steven, nothing's wrong at all. It's just that I was outside when Kevin Woolsey showed up. I...well, I guess I panicked."

Looking concerned, he stared at the young woman's face for a moment and then turned to Trask. "The reason I came up was to tell you that you have a man – a very big man – asking to see you. He's downstairs, with another fella, waiting on the front porch."

Wondering if the "Black Cat" had had a change of heart, he tipped his hat to Sweetie and said, "Come on, Randall. Let's go see who's come to call."

As the two older men took their leave, Steven asked, "May I sit and talk to you for a few minutes?"

Sweetie knew she was in for it, but she nodded. "Sure, Steven. Take a load off."

Her oldest friend took a seat by the far wall and said, "Sweetie, we don't have to go through with this, you know.

We could leave the Colonel and Randall behind to run this place and probably make a ton of money as simple investors."

Sweetie sighed. She loved Steven but he worried over her like a mother hen and sometimes she just wanted to kick him in the shins! She took a washrag out of the water basin and wiped the tears, dirt and sweat off her face and neck. Gazing at him in the looking glass, she said, "Steven, it was an over- reaction to a face I haven't seen in almost thirteen years, that's all. Don't worry, that's the last over-reaction you'll see out of me going forward."

Steven frowned. "I'm just saying…"

Sweetie frowned as well. "I know what you're trying to say, Steven, and *please* don't! I'll be fine, I promise. In a way, seeing him was a good thing because Kevin looks like the worst kind of thug. He was once the kinder of Billy's men, but if he's gone this rotten, I can only guess that the rest of his men are the worst kinds of crooks and bullies."

Steven shrugged. "Just trying to give you a last chance to back out, my friend."

She smiled, and answered, "I can't let it go, okay? I wouldn't if I could. Billy Drake is doing the same thing to dozens…maybe hundreds of people now that he once did to me and my family. He has to be stopped, and I want to be the one who stops him."

Steven gazed up at the girl he adored and then looked down at the floorboards. "I know, honey. Just know that, whatever happens, I will always have your back."

17

As Trask entered the dining room, he saw Tom Kirwin and an older gentleman seated at the back of the room. It looked like Ronny Stine, who was working in the bar today while his brother set up their upstairs apartment, had poured the men a couple of drinks.

He turned to Randall and murmured, "Looks like we're in luck."

Winters nodded, and asked, "I wonder who the other man is?"

"Let's go and find out," Trask said and waved at the two men before heading to the bar for his own drink. Ordering two neat whiskeys, he told Stine to put the guest's drinks on his own tab and then walked over to their table.

"Hello, good to see you made it," he said as he sat down.

They nodded and then Tom said, "Thank you for letting us in. I want to introduce you to my brother-in-law, Andrew Forsythe."

The man stood up and offered his hand to both Edwin

and Randall. Watching carefully, Trask noticed no hostility or racial rancor in the man's demeanor as he grasped Winter's hand, and immediately felt at ease. Whoever this guy was, and whatever his purpose here may be, he was not a bigot, and that weighed heavily in his favor.

"So," he said smiling, "How can we help you today?"

Tom cleared his throat. "First, I want to apologize for my behavior earlier at the gym. You're new to this town, I know, and although you've obviously learned a thing or two about the corruption around here, I don't think you know the half of it." He scowled down at his drink, and then picked his glass up and downed its contents.

Trask gestured to Stine for a bottle, and then said, "We have a pretty good sense of what's going on, although we don't know the victims personally – except for you and a few others, like Mister Stine and his brother."

Ronnie had just placed a bottle of whiskey on the table, and said, "Yeah, Tommy was once a good customer of ours back at the old place. Marty and I only lost our jobs, but Tommy lost his family's livelihood, and many good folks around here have lost everything, including their lives against this new mayor and his team of crooked cops." He nodded and took his leave.

Tom said, "I would like to take you up on your job offer, Mister Trask, if you'll still have me…"

Trask nodded and Winters smiled. "Of course, it still stands. We have need of a few good men and you fit the bill perfectly. When can you start?"

Tom replied, "Right now, if you like, but I have to fight on Friday night. Will that be a problem for you?"

Trask shook his head no and then turned to Andrew. "Mister Forsythe, did you want to hire on too?"

Andrew nodded. "You must be wondering why I'm here, right?" He looked at Trask and then Winters. "I'm not only Tommy's uncle, I'm also his handler. One of the reasons Tom was feeling riled this morning is that two nights ago, William Darcy's boxing manager, Otis Spank, came down to the gym and told Tom he had to throw the fight on Saturday." The man's cheeks turned red with wrath.

"Now," he added, "That's not unheard of, of course. Promoters do it all the time. But this was shaping up to be the biggest fight of Tommy's career and if he won, the cash prize would have netted at least a thousand dollars! That kind of dough would go a long way in keeping his kids fed, you understand. Now, he has to take a beating and will be lucky to see a quarter of the prize money...not to mention he'll lose his belt, which will postpone him from advancing on to bigger, better prize fights...at least for a while."

He looked Trask and Winters in the eyes and said, "I'm not naïve, gents, but enough is enough. When the mayor took my nephew's smithy, it almost brought his family, *no*, *my* family to its knees and pretty much left us destitute. We had a chance, with Tommy's hard work, to recoup our losses. But here comes Darcy again, taking all the cash to fill his own purse, just like he's done to so many other folks in this county, and devil take the hindmost."

He took a pull off his drink, and concluded, "I would like to help you take that bastard down, once and for all, if you'll have me. I am sort of a 'Jack of all trades', if you know what I mean. I'm handy with a gun, I'm a hard worker and I can read and write. Also, I have the gift of gab – at least that's what I've been told. And finally, I am a personal acquaintance of Darcy's."

He saw both Trask and his partner stiffen and stare at him with sharp eyes. Holding his hands in the air, he murmured, "Steady on, boys. I told you, I'm Tommy's manager, and mainly I deal with Spank, but once in a while, I run into Darcy. Sometimes, whether you respect a man or not, you have to deal with him.

"So far, my dealings have been, more or less, polite and somewhat profitable. Now, though, he's back to screwing me and mine, and that needs to stop!"

A dreadful grin took over Trask's face, and to Tom and Andrew's amazement, the mild-looking Negro man began to smile as well. "I have to say, gentlemen, we have been hatching a scheme that was missing only one component," Trask said. "An inside man. Now, it seems that we have found one. Welcome, Andrew. You're hired."

18

Friday dawned cool and overcast, and the Lucky Lady Saloon was in full roar with final preparations. The smell of good food filled the air, and pastries by the tens of dozens were being set by in the large pantry.

Sweetie and her partners felt like fifth wheels and wanted to escape the hustle, so they decided to head down to the boxing match being held at the Grange. They were a little early for the main feature starring The Black Cat and Darcy's man, Mighty Maxwell Cummings, but there were several lesser fights scheduled before the main event.

Feeling set-free, and surprisingly carefree, Sweetie stared about with big eyes at the mass of automobiles, buggies, carts and horses filling the parking area in front of the barn-like structure. The smell of popcorn, hot dogs, cider and beer filled the air, and throngs of people waiting in line to get in, seethed with excitement.

They take their boxing seriously here, Sweetie mused as Trask parked the buggy next to several other conveyances. A teenaged boy ran up and asked if they wanted full stable services while they watched the fights, or just water brought to their mounts on an hourly basis.

Knowing the animals were fresh, and that they would only be staying for two or three hours, he opted to keep the animals in the traces while they were inside and paid the boy to bring water and a bucket of oats for the team of two to share. The kid grinned, pocketed the tip and ran to fetch a bucket of oats.

The four of them ambled along the queue and heard snippets of discussion; "I heard that the odds are in favor of Mighty Max...", and "No way! The Cat will knock Max's head clean off!"

Many of the ladies in attendance wore their finest gowns and jewelry as if they were attending a high-society ball, and Sweetie saw a number of men exchanging cash with furtive smiles.

She smiled and then twitched slightly in discomfort. Lately, to keep her identity hidden, she'd taken to wearing a false mustache. The appendage did wonders in hiding her rich lips but itched like crazy. Still, she looked masculine enough with the fake facial hair, men's clothing and gold-framed spectacles.

Which was a good thing, as she could see that both Kevin Woolsey and Pete Meadows were sitting on stools at the ticket counter with rifles across their laps. They looked bored and Sweetie could see many people shy away nervously as they approached the ticket taker.

She moved closer to Steven, who murmured, "Heads up, Sweetie, looks like that Woolsey fellow again."

She replied, "Yes, and that's Pete Meadows sitting across from him."

Her escorts stiffened and gazed ahead at the two deputies. Just as Kevin had gotten heavier, almost obese over the years since that fateful day, Pete Meadows seemed to be carved down to the bone. His once handsome features were stretched tight across narrow cheekbones and his thin lips were turned down into a sour grimace.

She saw Kevin's gaze fall on her and her companions and watched as he turned to Meadows with his observations. Pete's eyes immediately turned their way again and he scowled as Trask stepped up to the ticket-taker with a broad grin. "Four seats up front, if you have 'em," he said.

The ticket taker glanced up and said, "Those are premium seats, Mister, and cost more..."

Trask asked, "How much more?"

The little man answered, "Two bucks a pop, sir, but that includes one free beer for each of you, and as many peanuts as you can eat."

"That's fine, my man. Give us those four seats, and we'll all be happy."

Sweetie was staring down at the ground, up at the sky and everywhere she could think of to avoid Pete and Kevin's eyes, which seemed to be drilling into her and her friends like 10-penny nails. Trask, however, was not impressed by the appraisal, and he said, "Well, Deputy, did you find The

Lucky Lady's paperwork in order?"

Kevin glared. "No problem with the licensing, Mister Trask, but we will be monitoring your business, rest assured."

There was no reason under the sun for such hostility on Kevin's part, but he oozed dislike and challenge while Pete continued to study them with pale, deadly eyes. Trask, undaunted, answered, "Well, monitor away, Deputy, you'll find the Lucky Lady to be a tough egg to crack, I think."

"Hmmm, I guess we'll see about that," Pete sneered, and startled a little as Trask narrowed his eyes. Suddenly, the starchy old man with mutton-chop whiskers looked a lot more formidable than he'd first thought...as did his companions. All four men stared at him as if they knew a secret that he was not privy to and his skin crawled with alarm.

Then, the moment passed. The four men passed the ticket counter and made their way inside the Grange building, as Pete and Kevin wondered why they suddenly felt so spooked.

***

Sweetie and her friends enjoyed the fights and watched with wise eyes as their man, Tom Kirwin, took a mighty fall in the fourth round of the featured fight. It wasn't even a very good performance.

The boxer known as Mighty Max kept a careful distance from the Black Cat's right jab; such a distance that Tom, bored of waiting for his opponent to step inside, kept urging the other boxer forward to put a hasty end to the farce, but to no avail.

Finally, Tom batted Max's gloves to the side, stepped into the man's arms and, lifting the boxer's left glove, aimed the man's fist at his own chin. It was hard to tell if the glove made contact, but Tom suddenly went down with a crash and Maxwell lifted his arms in victory.

There were plenty of groans from the audience and cash exchanged hands as Sweetie and her companions made their way outside. They were not alone. Most of the crowd had left when they did, and Trask could hear the bitter complaints of men who were sure the fight had been rigged in Maxwell's favor.

Of course, they're right on the money, Trask thought and then he looked up in alarm as he heard Sweetie gasp. "Oh no," she cried, "What happened to our horses?"

"Dammit!" Steven snarled as they came to a stop about ten paces from where they'd parked their buggy. The two matched bays were sprawled out on the ground dead. They were still bound to the traces and their struggles had canted the buggy forward, so it rested precariously on the front tongue. The horse's muzzles were shiny with blood and foam had formed and dried into a scrum on their mouths.

Sweetie wanted to weep but knew that no "real" man would succumb to tears at the loss of the animals, so she shut her mouth and let Trask rage. "What has happened here?" he demanded.

Winters murmured, "I'm betting those two deputies played a part in this, boss."

"Yes, but, HOW! How come no one saw this…this vandalism!"

Winters sighed. "Seems that this is the way of things around here. Hopefully, if we keep our wits about us, we can bring this sort of thing to an end."

Trask looked around, in vain, for the team of teenagers who had been hired to care for the customers mounts and seeing no trace of the boys, noticed that a crowd was forming around them – bystanders who'd heard Trask's explosion of rage and come to investigate.

Steven, who'd also noticed the growing crowd, ran over to hire a taxi. Coming back, he said, "We need to get out of here and most of all, Trask, we need to keep a low profile, okay?"

Edwin Trask, who was livid, swallowed his anger and said, "Yes, you're right. Let's get outta here." Then, under his breath he added, "I'll deal with those two deputies in my own way. Mark my words."

19

Sweetie stared in astonishment at the line of traffic outside The Lucky Lady Saloon that stretched down the road and around the block. She could actually only see about three hundred yards down the road, but Trask and Steven had assured her that the line stretched for over a mile with more vehicles joining the queue every minute. It was 2:30 in the afternoon, Saturday, and the establishment was slated to open their doors at 3:00.

Hearing rumors that the house would be full to overflowing, the crew had rented a number of buffet tables which were placed all around the back yard and, even now, the waitstaff was rushing to and fro, placing tablecloths and fresh flowers on the extra tables. Ron Stine was setting up a temporary bar by the back door, and Mrs. Bartonelli and her grandchildren were bringing trays of fresh pastries outside for the guests' pleasure.

Curtis Guthrie had opted for a pig roast, which was even now filling the air with heavenly aromas, but he also had racks of lamb and freshly caught salmon. There were huge bowls of salad, two giant cauldrons of Texas-style beans, and an assortment of fresh veggies which had arrived the day before from Southern California.

The staff was literally running from the kitchen to the backyard and she could hear Curtis issuing orders with military precision. Sweetie itched to lend a hand but Trask, waking up cranky from last night's activities in taking care of their dead horses, and towing their buggy back home, told her in no uncertain terms to *stay out of sight!*

So, she sat and watched as dozens of people, dressed to the nines, filed in the front door of her new establishment. They had hired a three-piece band and now a mixture of symphony pieces and a few assorted military tunes filled the golden afternoon air.

On one hand, her heart pounded in gratitude – a Grand Opening like this was every new business owner's dream. Unfortunately, she knew that this new venture was nothing more than an expedient end to a means. She could almost feel Billy Drake's hands closing over them.

Speaking of which…she sat up and peered through the sheer curtains at the arrival of a fancy burgundy coach with four matching blacks. Sweetie's eyes narrowed as she saw her old enemy step out of the pricey carriage along with a stately woman and two young girls. She smirked. The mayor, who now called himself William Darcy was also dressed to the teeth in a fancy black suit, gray, bowler-style hat and, honest-to-God white spats.

Thinking back on the day she was raped, and her father was shot to death in front of her eyes, Sweetie remembered the blank, distant look on Drake's face as his henchman, Eddie Machete did his worst. Her smirk turned into a grimace of rage. She wanted nothing more than to march downstairs with her gun in one hand and her sword in the other and lay him low.

Even as she grappled with her feelings, she knew the only thing *that* would accomplish was being hanged in the town square or spending the rest of her life in prison. If all went well, though, the plans she and her friends had painstakingly drawn up would ensure her enemies' incarceration, at least, not to mention Drake's downfall – both politically and economically.

She watched as Drake hobnobbed with the many people standing in line, and his wife blushed with pleasure as more than one gentleman doffed his hat and bowed over her white gloved hand. She was a pretty woman, and far too young for her old enemy but money talked in high society. Her young girls were also very pretty and were displaying splendid manners, although they seemed rather frightened and shy.

Shaking her head, Sweetie got up and stretched. She hated being kept out of the loop, and wondered how Trask's new hire, Andrew Forsythe, would do when he made his way to Drake's table. Steven had told her that the man possessed the 'gift of gab' and was a consummate actor, but she also knew that even the best stage actor could suffer a case of 'stage-fright'.

She paced back and forth as the noise level inside her new restaurant/saloon rose with every passing minute. Clenching her hands together, Sweetie Mack prayed that their scheme would bear fruit.

***

Tom (The Black Cat) Kirwin stood by the wall with his new co-worker, Bradley Gooding. He liked the kid, although he was still pretty green. Brad had taken one look at Tommy and said, "Uh, Mister Tommy, the bosses never said, but I hope you'll be the boss of security, instead of me. I'm game but I'm thinking that you got a better eye for trouble than I do."

Steven Mercer happened to be standing nearby, and at Brad's words, he turned and winked. His look suggested that he approved of the kid's suggestion, and Tommy said, "Sure thing, kid. I ain't your boss, though, okay? That's his job," he tipped his head at Steven. "Still, if things get rough around here, look to me for instructions. I won't steer you wrong."

Brad was exceedingly grateful that *he* was not the catbird in charge, especially now that William Darcy, that stinker of a mayor, and his dirty cops were holding court in the middle of the restaurant. As usual, Kevin Woolsey and Pete Meadows were staring about with angry, narrow eyes and making everyone in the general vicinity squirm.

Tom watched, as well, and couldn't help but notice

Darcy's eyes run all over the new restaurant; the house itself, the fine silk drapes, the snowy white tablecloths, the gleaming silver flatware, the crystal vases and glassware as if it all belonged to him. As if it were only a matter of time... and that time would be right quick if he had anything to say about it.

Tommy clenched his fists and heard young Bradley say, "What is it, Tommy? Trouble?"

Tommy swallowed his anger and shook his head. "Nah, not yet. But you'll be the first to know if it comes to that, okay?"

Brad leaned back against the wall and smiled. "Just you say the word, boss. Nothing I'd like better that to tip that old hoss right on his head!"

Tommy smirked in reply and watched as his uncle made his way to Darcy's table.

20

Andrew Forsythe adopted his normal expression of uppity servitude as he approached Darcy's table. He had found over the last few years that Darcy seemed to appreciate a certain amount of lip from his associates. Not too much, of course, but just enough that Darcy felt himself grow bigger in his largess. Too much humility, however, seemed to fuel Darcy's fury – as if he could not accept the fact that he inspired fear, rather than respect.

So, approaching with a smarmy grin, Forsythe extended his hand and said, "Mayor! I can't believe they let the likes of you in the door!"

Darcy smiled and replied, "The same could be said of you, my man. Say, isn't that bouncer your own nephew- the infamous Black Cat?"

Forsythe glanced toward the back wall and nodded. "Yup. The management approached Tommy a couple of days ago – said they needed a good man to run security around here. And, from the look of this turn-out, they weren't wrong."

Darcy studied the crowd and shrugged. "This is just a flash in the pan, I reckon. Give it a couple of months and this joint will be another flopped business. Most of the folks you see here today aren't going to leave the city proper to come clear out here for a bite to eat or a quick drink at the end of the day. Unless the owners of this joint have a *lot* of cash to spare, I figure they'll be out of business by year's end."

Andrew's spine tingled. Darcy had just given him the perfect opportunity to spring his trap. Casting his eyes about dramatically and making sure Darcy saw his furtive movements, Forsythe leaned over and whispered, "I heard tell that these folks are so rich, they're shipping wagon loads of gold and currency up by stage every other week! I can't help but think that kind of moola will go a long way in keeping this place afloat!"

Darcy's eyes sharpened and Forsythe rubbed his mental hands together in glee.

"Where did you hear this, Andrew?" Darcy asked.

Andrew looked over his shoulder again, and Darcy snapped, "Come over here by me and sit down, for pity's sake. If there was ever a man with a secret, it would be you, Andrew."

Forsythe grinned and said, "Sorry, William. I'm telling tales out of school, so to speak, and I don't want to get my nephew in any trouble..."

"What's Tom got to do with this?" Darcy asked.

Sitting down by Darcy's left side, Forsythe murmured, "I already told you that the owners hired my nephew on as chief security officer, right? Well, besides keeping the peace around here during business hours, he's expected to meet up with the coaches that are hauling money up here from California. It's supposed to be a secret, but Tommy told me about it... mainly so that if anything happens to him on one of those runs, I can step in to help take care of his two kids. He's a widower, ya know, and needs the cash to pay for a nanny."

Forsythe could see the mad gleam in Darcy's eyes as he pondered the idea of stagecoaches full of gold and cash. The mayor took a deep drink of the whiskey in his glass and asked, "So, how often do these stages come along?"

Forsythe shrugged. "Tommy heard that they show up every couple of weeks. Apparently, a coach showed up just this week...but not here, you know. There's a rendezvous point just outside of Spokane...ummm, a little place called, Grandview? Nah, that's not it. Granville! Yes, that's the place."

Darcy felt a thrill; that old familiar feeling of conquest that used to overtake him when he was a younger man. It wasn't as though he needed the money, not anymore. By anyone's standard, he was a wealthy man. No, it was the thrill of power that made his manhood stiffen and his blood boil. After all, these wealthy investors had moved into *his* town, without a by-your-leave- and made themselves at home.

Then, a niggling doubt entered his mind and he studied the boxing promoter with suspicious eyes. "Why are you telling me this, Andrew?"

Forsythe blushed as if caught out. "Well" he said. "This is my hometown, right? I've got no loyalty to these new folks, but I do have loyalty to my brother's son, Tommy. I guess I was thinking that if you got a favor from me, you might find your way to granting The Black Cat another shot at a prize match that would restore his belt; you know, sooner rather than later."

Darcy sneered, and then turned as his wife said, "Honey, it looks like they're bringing our meals...will you join us?" She aimed a pointed look in Forsythe's direction.

"Yes, my dear. My business associate was just taking his leave."

Andrew felt the jab and prayed that the fish had just swallowed the hook he'd cast. Standing up, he murmured, "Well, think about it, Mister Mayor, won't you?"

✳✳✳

Heart thudding with nerves, Andrew ambled over to where Tom stood by the wall. Stepping up next to the younger man, who was the spit of his own older brother, Forsythe stood next to his nephew, who asked, "How'd it go?"

Staring about at the many customers in the restaurant, the older man smiled pleasantly and answered, "He took the bait; hook, line and sinker...I think."

Looking anywhere besides Darcy's table, the two men observed the diners, the staff and the small sidebar where their new bosses stood chatting with a group of prominent businessmen. Forsythe really wanted to run up to Trask and tell the man of his success, but he'd been warned to play it cool, and he did not want to disappoint. Especially since he could actually see Darcy cutting glances at him out of the corner of his eye.

That old coot, he thought with disgust, *he doesn't trust a soul – because his own soul is as black as night.* Still, he acknowledged, the man was right to be suspicious. He'd just been set up, but Forsythe figured that Darcy would not be able to resist such a prize... *gold* and *banknotes* piled high in a coach just waiting to be snatched!

Forsythe's smile grew wider at the thought and then a ruckus broke out by the front door. It looked like two old bums were trying to force themselves inside the front doors and young Brad was attempting to force them back outside without causing too much of a scene.

"Excuse me, Uncle. I need to give the kid a hand," Tom said.

Forsythe watched as Tom made a beeline to the buffet table, spoke to a waitress and then walked to the front doors where the local townies were setting up a howl.

Andrew watched as a waitress filled two plates with food and then walked over to where his nephew was shepherding the bums outside with a quiet voice and the temptation of good, free food on two plates.

Tommy's a good lad, he mused...*and smart too. He just diverted a social catastrophe by a simple act of kindness.* He glanced over at Steven Mercer and saw that the man was watching quietly with a gentle smile of approval on his face.

Oh, Forsythe worried. *I sure hope these good folks can stop the mayor and his dirty cops from destroying what's left of this town. And, I hope they can bring those skunks down without getting themselves hurt in the process!*

PART THREE

MATTHEW WILCOX

21

Matthew Wilcox sat on a stump at the foot of his wife's grave, smoking a cigar and speaking softly into the late afternoon mist. Storm clouds had moved in a week earlier, bringing early morning rain showers and sudden after-noon squalls. The temperatures were warm, though, and Matthew was enjoying the respite from June's summer temperatures.

"Oh, I wish you could see him now, Iris! He's the very image of you…well, his reddish-blond hair anyway, and his eyebrows. He's built like me, though. He's tall – even taller than me, and he already out-weighs me by a good twenty pounds." Matthew smiled.

"Chance is home now, you know, and breaking every feminine heart in the county, too," Matthew sighed. "I've been talking to him about it. You know, being careful with those girls' hearts. I know he doesn't mean any harm, but there are already two girl's fighting over his attentions. He can't help that he can charm the birds right out of the trees, but he's going to get in trouble one of these days, so…" Matthew paused for a moment to relight his stogie.

"… so, I've been thinking about opening up a private investigation agency and hiring our son to be my partner. What do you think about that?" He stopped talking for a moment and listened intently to the quiet hush of his own little graveyard.

There were three graves – one for his wife Iris, one for his wolf, Bandit, and one for his littlest granddaughter, Polly, who had died in childbirth three years earlier. Iris' daughter, Abigale, had almost died giving birth to the little mite and still mourned her loss today.

Resuming his heart-to-heart with the love of his life, Matthew said, "I've been telling you about how boring the life of an attorney can be, right? I thought it would be a good way to fight crime without actually wearing the star, but the kind of work I'm getting is estate law and the like. It's like the people around here are hiring me to be their parent! It's like they're counting on me to be their conscience. Honestly, dear, I just can't stand it!"

His voice had risen and Chance, who was riding up behind his father, paused for a moment and listened to what Matthew had to say. He wouldn't dream of trespassing on his pa's private time with his mother, but although Iris had been murdered when he was only a boy, he missed her so terribly, he longed to be a part of his father's dialogue now.

Matthew must have sensed his presence, though, for he turned around and smiled at his son. "Chance! Good, I've been wanting to talk to you about an idea that's been spinning around in my brain. Take a seat." He gestured at one of the other tree stumps that sat at the foot of the three graves.

"Sure, Pa, but we better make it quick. The reason I came up here is that you have a visitor. She okay, though. Sarah's serving tea." Sarah was the wife of one of Matthew's oldest friends, Abner, who had given up being a lawman and worked now as his stepson, Sam's, hired hand.

Matthew raised an eyebrow. "Who is this visitor, do you know?"

Chance shrugged. "No, but she's really pretty – for an older lady."

Matthew rolled his eyes. "Well, this won't take long. Then we'll head down and talk to your pretty lady."

Chance blushed. His pa had been after him lately about being too loose with his affection for the fairer sex, but what was a man to do? He couldn't help it that the girls around town were drawn to him like flies to honey, could he? Besides he was only being polite. He hadn't even kissed a girl yet, unless you wanted to count Becky Whittaker, who'd been passing kisses around to every boy in sight at last year's Christmas jubilee.

Matthew stared out over the Ime's ranch and smiled. It was his ranch now, of course, since Iris had been murdered by bad outlaws, but he would always think of Iris as he viewed the tidy house, the two barns, the fruit trees and the many cattle, sheep and horses. His late wife had spilled her soul into this land, and he felt her presence everywhere.

Still, he was no farmer...or lawyer either, it seemed. He had lost too much and risked too much in his life as a lawman to pursue more policing. Not to mention, at forty-five years-old he was too long in the tooth. But he had a new idea. An idea that would keep him in the crime-fighting game, and maybe even keep his son out of mischief!

Turning to Chance, Matthew asked, "How do you feel about becoming a private eye?"

Chance's mouth dropped open, and his green eyes grew wide. "Me? What do I know about being an investigator?"

"Well, nothing yet, but I would teach you. Thing is, you're a military man. You know how to shoot, fence, ride, fight and track, don't you? I have the legal skills, and the connections we would need to track criminals down." Matthew lit a new cigar and grinned.

"You know, as well as I do, there's no room for you here on the ranch, and I'm sick of being an attorney. So, I thought we could go into business together. What do you think?"

Chance grinned and Matthew almost gasped at how like his mother he was. "God, Pa, that's a keen plan! I love it. When can we start?"

Matthew shook his head. "I'll get started on it right away, but there's still plenty to do before we hang a shingle. First off, I want you to shadow Roy and Dicky for a month or so, okay? They'll teach you what you need to know about the law. Then, when they say you're ready, we can advertise our services."

Chance's cheeks were glowing with excitement, and Matthew felt almost as thrilled as his son. His days as a country lawyer were coming to an end, and he was going to move forward with his life. Noting that a rainbow had formed over the valley in which Iris' farm nestled, he stood up, brushed off the seat of his pants and said, "For now, though, we'd better go see to the pretty lady, right?"

Chance grinned. "Well, she's way too old for me, Pa, but maybe she would suit you!"

Matthew shook his head, and murmured, "Let's head on down."

Man, and son mounted their horses and rode toward the house where Matthew could see a fine carriage parked by the aspen trees near the front entrance. Gazing into the sudden sunshine, he squinted at a very tall lady who was standing on the front porch with a cup of Sarah's tea in her hand.

He studied the woman's short hair and fine, rich clothing. He noticed her familiar, winsome smile, the high sharp cheekbones, periwinkle blue eyes and the way she held her head high in pride. But what he felt was akin to shock.

For what he saw standing in front of him now was an adult version of a little girl named Sweetie Mack, whom he'd met and tried to help a long time ago, when Iris was still alive. A little girl who had been brutalized by a band of deadly outlaws.

A woman grown now and standing on his own front porch with a charming smile on her face! Heart pounding with bitter-sweet memories, Matthew climbed down off his horse, and strode toward where she stood, with his arms outstretched in fond greeting.

22

Matthew wrapped his arms around Sweetie, who stiffened at first, and then relaxed into the embrace. She did not welcome physical affection, normally, (unless she was stinking drunk, which was vanishingly rare.) But Mr. Wilcox's arms felt like a cozy blanket, safe and warm.

She had been worried about their first meeting. Would the man even remember her? Would he resent the fact that she'd up and left, without saying goodbye or trying harder to express the gratitude she felt for his and his lovely wife's help? But one look at his face told her that Matthew Wilcox not only recognized her but was a good and decent man, through and through.

But what happened to Iris? she wondered. Sweetie had actually looked forward to connecting again with Matthew's wife more than Matthew himself; but when she asked the nice lady, Sarah Smalley, about where Iris was, the Indian woman had looked down and murmured, "You can ask Mister Matthew about that, okay?"

Sweetie stepped away from Matthew and said, "Hello, Mister Wilcox. It's so good to see you again."

Looking up, she was shocked to see tears gathering in the man's eyes, and she couldn't help but wonder if seeing her was bringing the man pain. He gazed back at her and grinned.

Wiping the sudden moisture away, he said, "Oh, Sweetie, forgive an old man for too much sentiment, alright? It's just that I've seen so many bad things happen to innocents, so often, seeing you now – a survivor – just made my day. Hell, my whole year!"

Matthew laughed and turned to a young man standing behind them. "Chance, come and meet an old friend of mine. She was a friend to you once, too, but you were probably too young to remember now."

Chance smiled and doffed his hat. Giving a slight, military bow, he murmured, "Chance Wilcox, ma'am, at your service."

Sweetie's eyes grew large and she burst out laughing. "My God, you were cute as a bug then, but look at you now! You must be breaking hearts all up and down this valley!"

Chance blushed and glanced over at his pa. "Well, ma'am. Honestly, I'm just being polite is all. How long ago was it that you met me and my pa?"

Sweetie frowned, and said, "I think you had just turned two, or maybe three years-old. I needed some help, and your folks took me in and gave me shelter. I stayed here on this very ranch and for a little while, you were my constant companion. I think you figured I was just another sister!"

Both Matthew and Chance laughed and then Matthew said, "Let's go up on the porch and have Sarah bring us some supper. What d'ya say?"

Smiling, Sweetie followed the older man up onto the wide veranda and sat down while Matthew stepped inside and asked Sarah to bring refreshments.

Curiosity got the better of her, and she decided to grab the bull by the horns. "Chance, where's your ma? I just loved Iris and was *so* looking forward to seeing her today."

Chance's face turned red and his wide lips turned down at the corners. Clearing his throat, Chance said, "Ma'am, my ma and my pa's pet wolf were murdered by a couple of bad outlaws, right here in this kitchen. It was a Deadman's Revenge..."

Sweetie turned pale and tears formed in her eyes. "Oh my God. I am so sorry. You could actually feel the love your folks felt for one another, and I always thought that, one day, maybe I'd be lucky enough to be a part of that same kind of love."

She sat silently for a moment and then asked, "Sorry, but what is a Deadman's Revenge?"

Matthew picked that moment to step back onto the porch. The big man said, "A 'Deadman's Revenge' is a slang term used amongst lawmen, Sweetie. It sometimes happens that an outlaw who's scheduled to hang will break free and go after the sheriff, deputy or marshal that caught him. Usually either the lawman or his family wind up in the crosshairs."

Matthew's eyes were dull, and his words had been spoken in a flat, emotionless manner. Chance winced as he saw Sweetie's question pierce his father's heart. Standing up, Chance stammered, "I'm sorry, Pa. It wasn't my place to tell, say anything..."

Then, Sweetie said, "Oh no, Mister Wilcox, it's my fault. I asked what had happened and he was too polite to ignore my question!" Then, she stood up and ran to Matthew, threw her arms around him and sobbed. "Oh, I'm so sorry that happened! Why does God have to take away everything that is good in this world... Why?"

Matthew had asked that same question many times himself, and still didn't have an answer, but feeling Sweetie's genuine remorse and sorrow, thawed some of the ice in his heart.

"He doesn't take everything, honey. Not everything! Look who's here with me – my son, and all of Iris' children are safe and sound, too. I even have a passel of grandchildren now, and they're the light of my life!"

Sweetie shuddered and took a deep breath. "I'm sorry, sir. Truly, I am." Pulling herself together, Sweetie gave a tremulous smile and said, "I came to you for a good reason, Mister Wilcox. Why don't we sit down and talk about what...I mean, *who* I found?"

Taking their seats, Matthew poured more tea, and said, "Sarah will be bringing luncheon out soon. In the meantime, who have you found?"

Sweetie sat back and Matthew watched as steel replaced sorrow in the woman's eyes. She grinned wickedly, and announced, "I found Billy Drake, Mister Wilcox. Him and all the others who murdered my pa and my uncle."

23

They sat and talked well into the evening, and although Sweetie had booked a room in one of the local hotels, Matthew insisted she stay the night. She really didn't want to intrude on Mr. Wilcox's privacy, but he seemed to genuinely want her there and to her surprise, she really wanted to stay.

Sweetie didn't realize it at the time, but when she had first taken shelter here on the Ime's ranch after the terrible things Billy Drake and his band of outlaws had done to her and her family, she had felt safe for the first time since her ma died.

Sure, she felt compelled to leave that safety behind, but now she knew that this place was indelibly imprinted on her heart and soul as a safe-haven from a frightful, perilous world.

Iris' son Samuel, and Sarah and her husband Abner joined them for dinner and after eating the cherry pie Sarah offered for dessert, they talked long into the darkening hours.

Matthew was somewhat shocked that this young lady had done so well for herself since she'd first fled Granville for Seattle and a start at a new life. He was also gratified that Sweetie had found a loyal friend in young Steven Mercer, whom he knew to be a very good and decent prosecutor for the citizens of King County in Seattle, Washington.

He asked at one point if there might be wedding bells for the two of them anytime soon, and Sweetie blushed to the roots of her hair. "No!" she exclaimed. Then, as if realizing that her protest was too severe, she added, "No, sir, it's not like that between us. Steven has his own interests, but we remain true and loyal friends."

Matthew's eyebrows crept up, but he kept silent. He had found himself wondering, even before he sent Sweetie Steven's way, if the young man might be a homosexual, and now it seemed his suspicions were correct. Still, he was glad that Sweetie had found a champion in her endeavors.

She told all of them about her business associates and what they were doing to wrangle Billy Drake, aka William Darcy, into the long arm of the law. She also explained how she'd been in disguise since arriving from California – which explained why her hair was cut unfashionably short and why her upper lip was slightly chapped from wearing a fake mustache.

Finally, she explained what they had put into play last Saturday night at the grand opening of her new saloon/ restaurant. "So," she finished. "we will put a bug in Drake's ear about a week from now. We'll tell him a new shipment of gold and currency will be arriving by coach at the stage-line office just outside of Granville. Hopefully, Drake will take the bait and maybe, with your help, we can stop him once and for all."

She paused for a moment, as if weighing the wisdom of full disclosure and then said, "I have worked hard on this sir, but some of the things me and my partners have done are not quite...um, legal. If I share information with you now, can you promise you won't turn me and my people into the local law?"

She studied Matthew's features looking for either censor, or approval. Seeing neither on Matthew's face, she grew nervous and said, "Sir, you don't need to be involved at all, of course. I guess, I just assumed you were still a sheriff and would be keen on bringing down an old outlaw gang. But, since you're retired, I should just let you off the hook."

Matthew grinned and shook his head. "First off, please call me Matthew, okay? I appreciate the respect you show your elders, but I'm starting to feel as old as Methuselah!"

Soft laughter filled the air and Sweetie grinned. "Matthew it is, sir!"

Matthew sat back in his chair. "I may be retired, Sweetie, but that doesn't mean I'm dead and buried. The answer to your question is *Yes*, you can trust us to keep your council – just so long as your deeds don't cross the line into outright theft or murder. Deal?"

Sweetie nodded. "Deal. Actually that is exactly what

we're trying to avoid, Matthew. Drake is too powerful to try and take the law into our own hands. He's got most of the policemen bought and paid for in the Wenatchee area, which is why we decided to bring the stage here. Also, Steven thinks that two out of the three judges in Chelan County are in his pocket as well. No, what we are doing is a trick, see? There *will* be a stagecoach filled with gold and bank notes, but the notes are forgeries." She cleared her throat and searched Matthew's eyes. "That's why I'm asking for your discretion. My team and I know that forging money is illegal, see?"

Matthew nodded, replying, "No problem, so far, Sweetie."

Sweetie smiled and continued, "The gold is actually gold-painted lead, so the big payload Drake is counting on is fake. The problem is Billy's men won't know that and I'm afraid they'll come in guns blazing. What I'm hoping for is some sort of back-up. Men you know who are good at protecting themselves when Drake's boys come after the loot."

"Ah!" Matthew grinned. "That's why you came to me. We're right here in Spokane County where I know and am friends with most of the lawmen."

Sweetie blushed. "Now you're making me feel like I think your friends are dispensable! I don't feel that way at all, you know. It's just that the men who work for me are not gunfighters. They are shopkeepers and family men. I know from my research that many Spokane County sheriffs and deputies are well respected, even feared for their fighting skills."

Matthew laughed. "Whoa, Sweetie. I don't think you're heartless, at all. In fact, I think you're very smart. What you need on that stage are men who can and will protect themselves against road agents, and if you're correct, it sounds like Drake's men will send some tough hombres to the task."

Sweetie nodded. "Yes. I'm hoping he'll send Kevin Woolsey and Pete Meadows, but maybe that's just wishful thinking. Still, a lot of nasty men work for Billy and whoever he sends will be bad to the bone."

She sighed. "My partners and I feel that if we can take alive the men Billy sends, they'll sing like birds once they're away from Wenatchee. Matthew, I'm almost a hundred percent certain that Drake will come after the gold and banknotes we've waved under his nose like a couple of big, fat carrots, but I don't want anyone to get hurt in the process. Do you think you can help us?"

Matthew grinned. "Your plan has a few holes in it, but I like it, so far. I remember what Billy Drake was like back when you were just a kid. Those crooks not only did you and yours harm, they hurt a lot of other people in Spokane County before they gave us the slip." He rubbed his hands over his face for a few moments and then said, "I would have kept after them, but trouble came my way, right here on my own doorstep." He reached over and placed his hand on Chance's shoulder.

"Trust me, I was in no condition to do anything other than bring those men to justice, and that almost destroyed me...me *and* my family." He sighed. "Anyway, I've been making do as a lawyer the last few years. Oddly enough, my son and I were just, today, developing a plan to start up a new detective agency in this area."

Sam, Iris' oldest son, sat up straight and blurted, "Pa! When were you going to let me in on this new plan of yours?"

Matthew held his hands up in surrender, "Hold up there, son. Nothing has been finalized. Hell, it hasn't even begun yet. Chance and I were simply thinking on it. But..." his green eyes, which were just as beautiful now as when he was a boy, gleamed in the porch light. "...this may just be the perfect place to start."

Chance asked, "What are you thinking, Pa?"

Matthew pinched his chin – a trademark body movement signifying deep concentration. "Don't rightly know yet, son." Looking at Sweetie's angular but pretty face, he added, "But I *do* know a lot of lawful pistol-men in these parts, and many of them will surely recall that owlhoot, Billy Drake."

He frowned. "Just the idea of that man profiting from the blood and tears of his past deeds makes me sick!" He stood up abruptly and stepped down into the yard as the others watched.

He paced back and forth, one fist beating the other as he remembered all the other bad outlaws he'd tracked down over the years. To a man, those crooks had stolen other people's hopes and dreams whether they be rich or poor. It was as if they were either too lazy or just too greedy to make it on their own merits. He was done with it!

Turning back to Sweetie, and his friends and family, he said, "I'm in, Sweetie. I no longer wear a badge, but I know good men who do. I'm sure, with a lot of help and good planning we can cut those crooks off at the knees, and wouldn't that be just fine?"

24

Sweetie woke up in Matthew's guest room and stared at the ceiling for a moment. A faint smile etched her lips as she recalled the discussion last night. Her hard-wrought plans were coming to fruition! She had no way of knowing whether the outcome would be favorable, though. After all, Billy's army of bad players was huge, and corruption filled his territory like a disease.

Still, she now had an army of her own. A much smaller one, perhaps, but a righteous group of lawmen was coming to her aid in bringing down her enemy, and her heart swelled with joy. Maybe…finally, her pa and uncle would be avenged, and the sick fear which had filled her soul for so long could rise up and blow away on the summer breeze.

She rose up out of bed and stepped over to the window. Storm clouds had settled over Eastern Washington like a brooding hen the last couple of weeks, but had, apparently, flown away overnight leaving the sky as blue and bright as a robin's egg.

She stared down and watched as Matthew's son Sam, and Abner Smalley saddled up a couple of horses for their day's work. Then, as she watched, two riders approached the ranch from the main road. She squinted into the rising sun and saw a bright flash of metal on one of the men's chest. She wondered if Granville's sheriff, Roy Bean, and his deputy, Dicky McNulty had arrived.

Whirling around in excitement, Sweetie made for a chest of drawers where a wash basin and soap sat waiting. She made her toilet quickly and dressed in jeans and a long-sleeved shirt. Although trying to mimic a man was a pain, she did appreciate the freedom of pants over skirts. Besides, she was heading back to Wenatchee today, and she needed to be in disguise when she returned.

Hearing footsteps in the hallway outside her door, Sweetie heard Sarah call out, "Miss Sweetie, breakfast is served, and Mister Matthew wants you to come down and meet his friends."

Sweetie answered, "I'll be right down, Sarah. Thank you!"

A couple of minutes later, Sweetie clattered down the stairs in her high-topped leather boots and followed her nose to the dining room. When she entered, Matthew and his guests rose and gave her a slight bow.

She blushed, and murmured, "Oh, please. Sit down, gents." Then, remembering the man who had tried to help her when she was still just a child, she smiled and walked over to shake his hand. "Mr. Bean! I'm so happy to meet you again! And, Mr. ....?"

The younger of the two men smiled and shrugged. "My name is Dicky McNulty, ma'am. I wasn't around when you first met Matthew, but I know all about that bad gang that hurt you and your family."

Sweetie smiled at the little ginger-haired man and shook his hand. "Very pleased to make your acquaintance, Mister McNulty. You must be a very fine person, if you work with Matthew and Roy."

Dicky grinned, "Well, if anything, they made me what I am today."

Matthew laughed and said, "There's food and coffee on the sideboard, Sweetie. Get something to eat and join us, won't you?"

Sweetie was famished and filled her plate with scrambled eggs, bacon and toast. As she served herself breakfast, she could hear Matthew telling the two lawmen about Billy Drake and about how he had moved in and taken over the Wenatchee area. As she sat down at the table, she saw the sour expression on Sheriff Bean's face.

He glanced her way and grumbled, "Bet that just chaps yer hide, don't it?"

Sweetie couldn't help but grin, but she answered, "Oh yes, Roy. It really does."

Sitting back, Roy wiped his mustache and said, "Well, Matthew, what do you propose we do about it?"

For the next two hours, Sweetie and the men tossed around ideas about the illicit stagecoach and the best way to apprehend the robbers that would come gunning for it. To Sweetie's delight, Matthew's friends seemed almost as eager to bring Drake down as she was.

Questions were asked and answered, and schemes were proposed, until, finally, it was decided that Dicky, Chance and Abner would meet the stage in Seattle and ride back on it to the rendezvous point outside of Granville.

"But," Sweetie's nerves grew taut in alarm. "Matthew, your own son? What if he's hurt, or even killed? My heart couldn't take it!"

Matthew's green eyes regarded her, and he said, "Both Chance and Dicky are crack shots, Sweetie. Chance has spent the better part of his youth in military school and Dicky here, well, no one knows how he got to be such a good shooter, but put him up against just about anyone, and he'll put their lights out in a gunfight."

"Meanwhile" Roy continued, "the rest of us will be scattered around hiding behind boulders and trees. When the bandits come riding in, there's a good chance we can stop them before they get to within fifty-feet or shooting distance from the coach."

So, Sweetie thought, *Dicky would steer the horses, Chance would ride shotgun, and Abner would be sitting inside guarding the loot. Two crack-shots riding outside, and a huge, hulking man inside to add extra protection against attack. At least half a dozen assorted lawmen hiding outside and all of them ready, willing and able to stop any outlaw tempted to take my fake money.*

She had to admit, the plan sounded good. But she was no fool, and she understood how even the best-laid plans could go awry. Matthew studied her face and read her expression correctly.

"Sweetie, speaking as an old lawman, plans *can* go wrong. Even the best posse can suffer casualties, if they're not careful. But the team we're putting together this morning is of the highest quality, okay? Honestly, we could put those skunks down as easy as pie; that's how good both Chance and Dicky are with their guns, but the goal is to take them alive to, hopefully, turn State's evidence."

Matthew took a sip of his coffee, and then smiled. "My hope is that as soon as those boys see that they are surrounded on all sides, they'll throw their guns down and surrender peacefully."

Casting her doubts aside, Sweetie smiled and said, "It sounds like a good plan, Matthew." Turning to the other men, she added, "Thank you, fellas. Maybe, finally, we can bring Billy Drake to justice."

Frowning slightly, Sweetie asked, "Where is Chance, sir?"

Matthew grinned. "Oh, he hopped the morning train to Spokane. His job is to recruit some city law dogs as back-up in our plans."

Sweetie nodded, "Speaking of hopping trains, I need to find out when the next train leaves for Wenatchee. I told my partners I'd be back today..."

Matthew shook his head. "Sweetie, this is one area that

we'd like to see a change. Please, stay on here at the ranch. I actually think you got lucky that Billy didn't remember you last week. After all, I had you pegged the moment I set eyes on you."

His eyes bored into her soul for a moment and then he added, "In addition, the next week or so will probably be pretty quiet, but once this stage robbery goes South, things will change. You and your partners will be sitting ducks when Billy Drake finds out he's been set-up."

Sweetie's eyes grew large. "But...but I can't just leave my friends to do all my work for me. This is all my doing, Matthew. What would they think if I up and hid behind your skirts, while they take all the risks?"

Just then, the phone rang, and Sweetie jumped in her chair. "What the..." she gasped.

Matthew smiled. "We had a telephone installed a few months ago. Cost a fortune, but it's been well worth it."

A moment later, Sarah stuck her head around the door and said, "Mister Matthew, it's Chance calling for you."

Matthew winked at Sweetie, wiped his lips with a napkin and stood up. "Think about it, Sweetie. With a phone on the premises, you can keep in close contact with your partners while this sting goes down. I have a feeling your friends are with you now, not because of any monetary gain but because they really care about you. I also have the feeling that they would heartily agree with you staying here while our plans take root."

Then, he tossed his napkin down and strode out of the room to answer the phone.

25

Approximately 180 miles away, Trask frowned into his cup of coffee. Their newly installed telephone had rung, and he spoke to Sweetie about her and her friend, Matthew's, plans for the heist. He approved whole-heartedly.

He shifted irritably. His butt was sore from having a boot planted in it last night, and he wondered how the rest of his security team felt this morning. Glaring, he stared at Tommy's scrawled list of names – men who wanted to join the team.

The first few days after opening their doors, the crowds were mellow and sedate. But on day three a crowd of ruffians had showed up and caused as much mayhem as they could before being kicked to the curb. Trask thought, at the time, that those boys were a part of a cattle drive, or a bunch of local farm boys, bored and looking to let off some steam.

Since that night, however, more and more roughnecks and bullies came on a nightly basis. They weren't even trying to hide their intentions now. That first night the men had worn old but serviceable suits and ties before setting to – now the gangs just barged in, filthy and drunk, saps and leather straps in hand.

Trask rubbed his face in exhaustion. It was Drake's doing; he knew it in his soul. He didn't know if it was sheer meanness on the man's part, or if he was angry and jealous of a new business that had moved in, uninvited, to eclipse his own concerns. Either way, it was becoming a real problem.

Custom had dropped by half. Their tonier customers were keeping their distance as if afraid of catching William Darcy's notice, and the less affluent were simply afraid of getting their asses busted by William's bully boys. It was maddening! In business less than a week and already it was looking as though The Lucky Lady's luck had run out.

So, I'm about to hire two more men for my security team. More security, and a big reduction in prices might keep this sham alive long enough for Sweetie's sting operation to bear fruit. Might... Trask sighed in disgust.

He was happy, though, that Matthew Wilcox had talked Sweetie into staying on at his ranch. Sweetie was sure that she appeared "mannish", but she was dead-wrong. Although she was quite tall and muscular for a lady, there was just no disguising her frail bone structure and delicate features. At least this way, the men on her side of things could smash a few heads together without stepping on her feminine sensibilities or putting her at risk.

Trask wished he could meet this Matthew feller to see if he was on the level, but he had already spoken to a few law dogs in the Spokane area, who assured him that Wilcox was a straight shooter, who had devoted most of his adult life to keeping innocent people as safe as possible against the criminal element that seemed to flourish with the advent of automobiles and high-speed trains.

He hissed in exasperation as the sound of raised voices drifted upstairs from the restaurant/bar area. *For pity's sake! he thought, only 1:30 in the afternoon and the hurly-burley boys are making an appearance!*

Hearing a hush, Trask realized that Tommy and Bradley had made short work of the latest intrusion, but he despaired. He had signed on with Sweetie Mack for the money and an elevated sense of usefulness in his senior years. Somewhere along the way, though, he began to care deeply for the young woman – as a father would care for a daughter, for sure, but that made his devotion no less impactful. The fact that he hadn't yet been able to put a stop to Drake's daily assaults pricked his pride and made him wonder if he was truly up to the task of being Sweetie's head of security.

Another source of worry... Steven Mercer. As a younger man, Trask might have despised the lawyer for his womanly ways, his almost willful lack of fighting skills, and for the way Steven spent his private time. But time had mellowed his measure of a man. Thinking back on his time in the Army, Trask remembered that many homosexual men had served under him with pride and dignity, and some of those same men were his fiercest fighters.

Sadly, Steven was no fighter. He did, however, adore Sweetie Mack and preferred to fight for their mutual employer with a pen rather than a sword. Knowing that Steven was feeling both fearful and useless right now – as Trask fought to keep Sweetie's investment intact – he made a sudden decision.

Standing up, he strode to the door and walked down the hallway to Steven's room/office. Knocking on the door, he said, "Steven, are you in there?"

Trask heard the rustle of papers and then footsteps. The door opened and Steven peered out at him. "Hi, Edwin. Did you need me?" he asked.

Trask shook his head. "I don't, but I think Sweetie does. How would you like to take a trip up to Granville?"

✱✱✱

As Steven boarded the train for the Spokane area, William Darcy, aka Billy Drake held a meeting with his top lieutenants. Four men sat at Billy's fine cherrywood dining table sipping coffee and trying hard not to devour the French pastries arrayed before them, like pigs at a trough.

Kevin Woolsey and Pete Meadows did the best job of acting like highbrows at a tea party. After all, they'd been with Drake since they were only sprouts, and had partaken, along with their boss, of the good times as well as the bad. For now, French pastries were a given in this time of plenty.

For the other two men, however, the scrumptious treats were an almost unbearable temptation. They had been hired because they were tough, smart, and above all, hungry for success. It didn't matter to them that Darcy had originally been the instrument of their family's downfall. The only thing that mattered to them now was the fact that the same man was key to their survival.

Their names were Denny Carmichael and Roger Hampsted, and they stuffed their mouths with chocolate donuts and French vanilla cream cakes as Pete and Kevin watched in scorn. Finally, Pete could stand no more and he barked, "Hey Fattie, have you heard a word the boss said?"

This was addressed to Denny, who was close to topping 250 pounds despite the fact that his wife and daughters were close to starving at home. He stopped eating and blushed as he realized that he'd already eaten three out of the six pastries arranged on the china plate in the middle of the table.

Wiping his mouth and chin whiskers, he stammered, "Yes! I'm sorry, sir, but I did hear you say we're supposed to rob a coach sometime next week. That's right, ain't it?"

Darcy sneered. "I guess your ears still hear, Denny, despite the fact you're stuffing them with dough batter."

Carmichael pushed away from the table slightly, a certain amount of manly pride coloring his cheeks. "I *am* sorry, sir. I do love to eat, and there have been plenty of hungry days these last few years. I'm all ears though, okay? When will we do the deed?"

Roger Hampsted had stopped eating as soon as Meadows opened his mouth, and sat as still as a spider in its web. He even looked a little spider-ish with his thin black hair, stick-like arms and legs, and loose red-lipped mouth. Of the two men, Billy knew that Hampsted was the more dangerous; cold-blooded and filled with rage, a little like his old friend Eddie Machete, whom he missed to this day.

He was reminded, briefly, of that little slash Sweetie Mack, and wished as always that he had dispatched her to a quick death when her father, Dean had ended Eddie's life.

Sighing, Billy studied the faces of the men around him. He knew, without a doubt, that he did not need to rob that stage of its gold and paper notes. He had enough money, clout and prestige to carry him to the end of his days on earth.

Still, his fingers itched to rob the owners of the Lucky Lady Saloon. As he'd sat at one of their tables that opening night, and peeked over at the new owners, he sensed a nobility within them that he knew he'd never achieve, even if he lived to be a hundred and one years old.

He spoke then, saying, "Forsythe was talking to Tommy the other night, who said that the coach in question will be coming in from the Seattle area Thursday next. I want the four of you to intercept it a couple of miles before they hit the station."

Pointing at Hampsted, he said, "You and Denny will be the front men on this job. Ride in, disable the driver and whoever he has along with him as back-up, take the loot and then ride back to Pete and Kevin." He grinned, adding,

"Then you'll hand over the loot, and ride back home."

Carmichael asked, "Why do we have to haul the dough back to them? We could bring it straight to you without all the back-peddling!"

Darcy's face turned red, and he snapped, "Are you questioning my methods, Denny? Are you?"

Carmichael's eyes got big and he stammered, "Why, no, sir, not at all. I guess you have a better plan, right?"

Darcy snarled, "You can bet on it, buddy. This is a four-man operation, okay? You can either go along with it or find a new employer!"

Hanging his head, Carmichael went silent, and Darcy continued. "Pete and Kevin will be taking the gold and banknotes on to Seattle and hand it over to a middle-man. An old buddy of mine, named Sammy Chen. That's why this operation needs four men, Denny. You satisfied?"

Blushing wretchedly, Carmichael nodded and watched as his new boss sat back in his chair like a big, ginger cat. *A cat has a tail, though,* he thought resentfully, *maybe, one of these days when I make it rich, I'll pull it for him!*

Billy Drake sat silently for a moment and then he fished in his pocket and handed a ten dollar note to his henchmen, Carmichael and Hampsted. He figured he'd used enough stick to press his point home. Now, it was time for the carrot. "Here," he said with a smile. "Why don't you boys have lunch on me and while you're at it, get yourselves a couple of new hats. Yours are a little...uh, long in the tooth."

Carmichael stepped forward eagerly, but Hampsted's

dead gray eyes simmered with resentment. He hated being disrespected, always had, and Darcy's scorn was palpable.

In addition, he smelled a rat. Darcy's plan seemed to be some kind of trick, although he wasn't sure who the trick was being played on. *Still,* he thought with a mental shrug. *I might as well get as much out of the creep as humanly possible, while the pickin's are good.*

Hampsted had a sneaking feeling that Darcy's days were numbered. He'd almost always known when things were about to go south – maybe it was an inherited ability from his gypsy mother, or just a lifetime of experience whispering in his ear. But, as soon as he got his hands on the gold and cash in that coach, he would fly on out of there, and head for the hills.

He'd probably have to kill Carmichael on his way out, but that didn't bother him in the slightest. He'd seen the man's wife and daughters and the home (shack, rather) they were kept in and knew he wouldn't treat even a dog as harshly as Denny treated his family. Denny was a loser and would not stand in his way as he made his exit, *stage* left, from Wenatchee.

Chortling at his own wit, Hampsted doffed his hat and smiled as he followed Carmichael out of Darcy's dining room and out into the street.

26

Steven Mercer stepped off the train at the Spokane loco-motive depot and spotted Sweetie standing next to two tall men. One was older, distinguished looking and had graying, blond hair. Steven smiled, thinking, *Matthew Wilcox is looking well in his older years; almost the same as when we first met, twelve years ago.* The younger man had reddish-blond hair, but the same posture and look about the eyes and brow. *That must be Matthew's son, Chance,* Steven decided.

Sweetie looked very pretty in her flower-sprigged summer dress and smart hat, and her smile was brilliant with what seemed like true hope and joy. Steven realised he'd never really seen that kind of smile on her face before, and his heart lifted.

Striding toward them, he held his right hand out to shake. "Hello, Sweetie," he grinned. "You're looking well."

She ignored his outstretched hand and hugged him instead. "Hi, Steven! I am well, thank you. Steven, let me introduce you to the man who rescued me so long ago. I don't know what would have become of me without Mister Wilcox's help."

Steven grasped Matthew's hand and said, "Mister Wilcox! So glad to see you again. You are looking well, sir."

Matthew grinned in reply, "It's Matthew to you, Steven. I see you took very good care of our mutual friend."

Steven shrugged. "She's a hard one to resist, sir. She says jump and I just ask, 'How high?'"

Sweetie laughed. "That's hardly true, Steven, and you know it!" Shaking her head, she turned to Chance and added, "And, this is Matthew's son, Chance Wilcox."

The two men exchanged greetings and then Matthew murmured, "We should get in the car and head for home, okay? There may be eyes on us…"

Feeling a chill and resisting the urge to look over his shoulder, Steven picked his satchel up and said, "You're right, sir. I'm only now finding out just how much power Darcy holds in the Wenatchee area. It wouldn't surprise me a bit to find he has spies here as well as there."

The four of them made their way to a handsome, black automobile then made their way northwest, out of town. It was a fairly long drive to Matthew's home, about three hours, but they stopped twice… once for a nature-break and once for a picnic lunch in a pretty, flower-filled meadow.

Chance pulled fried chicken, potato salad, biscuits and peach preserve out of a wicker hamper and they set-to as Matthew filled Steven in on their plans. It all sounded good to him, especially since those plans did not seem to involve Sweetie at all. He was, frankly, relieved that Matthew had somehow talked Sweetie out of exacting her own, personal, revenge.

Sure, she was skilled in the art of war, but Steven felt that a certain, cold-blooded cruelty was key to a warrior's success and he didn't think Sweetie was cruel at heart. He acknowledged that she might prevail in a fair fight, but there was no way that her nemesis, Billy Drake, would fight fair.

When asked, Steven told them what William Darcy was up to in Wenatchee, or more specifically, The Lucky Lady Saloon. Sweetie gasped in outrage. "So," she hissed. "it's basically a shake-down...a protection racket using hard-arm tactics for a pay-off?"

Steven nodded. "Yes, but don't worry. Trask has things in order, at least, so far." He studied her face, adding, "It's costing a fortune, though. We are having to pay almost three times the going rate for security officers. Plus, the repair bills are piling up. Three nights ago, a couple of knife sharps pulled their blades inside the bar. Tommy and his men managed to subdue them, but two of those men were cut up; one pretty badly."

Sweetie frowned. "We *are* paying their medical bills, right? I know these men are, unfortunately, caught in the middle of a battle between myself and Billy Drake. I hate to think they are suffering because of me."

Steven said, "Yes, we are, but the one badly injured

man… he lost most of his nose and half an ear when he went up against the knife-man…Still," he shook his head, "you can't think that way, Sweetie. Each and every one of the men we've hired are aware of the risk. Many of them are in it for the pay, but quite a few of them are in it for their own revenge. Drake, or Darcy as I should say, has done a lot of harm to innocent citizens in Chelan County over the last ten years. Noah Shillings, the man who lost his nose, seems right proud of his scars just because he got them for standing up to William Darcy."

Looking doubtful, Sweetie stared off into the distance, and the hollow look that had shadowed her face since Steven had first met her, returned in the warm afternoon light.

Matthew started gathering up their picnic plates, and Steven pitched in to help. "Tell me, Matthew, when is this heist going to take place?"

Matthew glanced over at the younger man, and replied, "Next Thursday. We spent the better part of the morning in Spokane confirming the help of about a half a dozen deputies. All good shots, and all of them eager to see the end of Billy Drake and his gang's reign of terror."

Steven nodded. "Yes, that's what I'd heard, as well. Just, be informed, sir, William Darcy is a sly old fox. Seems to me like he's been one step ahead of us since we arrived. I'd hate to see him get the drop on all of you, too. I have no doubt that, if threatened, he'd see all of you dead without a qualm."

Matthew smiled, and something in the man's eyes chilled

Steven's soul. "Well, I have a few tricks up my sleeve, as well, Steven. I think it's high time that skunk goes down for the count, don't you?"

*∗∗

As Matthew and his friends climbed back in the car and drove home, Darcy addressed his two remaining lieutenants. "Okay, gents. I reckon you already know that those two clowns are just pawns in this game, right?"

They did know something was up – whenever Billy started scheming, his pale blue eyes got a far-away look to them, almost as if he was listening to a silent but imperative voice from some distant land.

Kevin asked, "Yessir, but what is the game, exactly?"

Darcy grinned. "I've been doing some figuring and have made a few telephone calls. Forsythe says that stage is coming by way of Seattle, and there are about twenty to twenty-five stage depots in the Seattle area. Tomorrow, I'm sending you two, along with five other men to case the joints. I want you to find out which stagecoaches are slated to head east next Tuesday, Wednesday and Thursday."

Darcy stopped talking and rooted around in his desk drawer for a moment. Then, he found a fat envelope and placed it in front of the men. "This envelope is filled with running money, a couple of maps and the names of bankers that are in my employ. I have also reserved and paid for a couple of hotel rooms in the city. They are in separate hotels, okay? I don't want people to see that you are actually working together."

He gazed at them as they nodded their heads in acknowledgment. Then he said, "I want you to figure out which one of those stagecoaches has got the dough, and then I want you to relieve them of their burden. The sooner you can do that, the less risk there will be of tracking the heist back to me… and by me, I mean *us*! Understand?"

Pete was grinning by now and Kevin nodded his head in appreciation. Still, he felt compelled to ask, "Billy, why involve Carmichael and Hampsted at all?"

Darcy shrugged. "Those boys are a losing proposition. I hired them to do some dirty work for me, but they're too rough and, by now, they know too much. I have men standing by who will get rid of their bodies as soon as they hit the Spokane area."

Pete was stunned. He had just been thinking that Hampsted was a thoroughly dangerous man. *Takes one to know one,* he thought. He'd glimpsed something coiled up and squirming behind Hampsted's eyes and felt relief that his boss had seen it as well and was acting on it.

"So," Darcy continued, "both of you will be acting independently of each other. Kevin…" he glanced at the heavy-set man. "three of the five men will be in your hotel. You will be their acting boss. And, Pete, the other two will be with you. As soon as you find that coach, call me and I'll send reinforcements. I want every penny that's in it, and I want you to bring it back to me. I'll be waiting for it at my apartment on 5th Street in Seattle, okay?"

He sat back in his chair and smiled. "You boys do a good job on this, and you'll get half the take."

Seeing the shock on their faces, he shrugged. "I don't really need the money, you know. I just want to take it away from those idiots at The Lucky Lady."

And with those words, he burst out laughing.

PART FOUR

THE TONG

27

Seattle detective, Dan Davis was sorting through his inbox, trying to organize his weekly notes into something his chief of police could understand, when the phone rang.

When the department had first sprung for telephones he was as excited as the next guy. After all, a quick phone call enabled him and his co-workers to move quickly, much more quickly than before, and had become an invaluable tool in their fight against crime in the city. Still, the infernal device never stopped squawking, and half the time he found himself fielding phone calls rather than doing the work he'd been hired to do.

Vowing to approach his boss, once again, about hiring a secretary to man the phones, he glared at the black device and picked up the handset. "Seattle police department, how may I help you?"

He then heard a voice he hadn't heard in years. "Dan? Is this Dan Davis?"

Dan smiled and said, "Yes sir, it is. How are you, Mister

Wilcox? Long time no hear!"

Many years before, Dan had met the sheriff of Granville, Washington, Matthew Wilcox, when he'd come to Seattle to track down his wife's murderer. Although his boss at that time had thought Wilcox was an impertinent and dangerous man, almost an outlaw himself, Dan had felt the lawman was simply heartbroken and fixated on getting justice for his deceased wife.

They'd struck up a friendship and had kept in touch over the years. It was a bit of a shock to hear Matthew's voice now, however. Last he'd heard, Matthew had hung up his star and gone into lawyer work, choosing apparently, to fight bad guys from behind a desk rather than the back of a horse.

Matthew answered, "Oh, I'm just fine, son. And you? How many kids do you have now?"

Dan blushed. He'd married four years ago, and his wife had proven to be quite fertile; the four children running around his house proved that fact. He was both proud of and slightly embarrassed by his wedded bliss and abundant progeny. He laughed into the handset. "Four kids now, sir, although my wife and I are taking precautions against too many mouths to feed."

Matthew chuckled, "Good luck with that, Dan. Kids are a man's principle blessing. Nice to know there's someone, or in your case, many someone's to help you out in your old age."

Knowing Matthew hadn't just called to shoot the breeze,

he asked, "Sir, you never call me directly, you always write letters instead. Is there something you need?"

The line grew silent, although Dan could hear light breathing on the other end. Finally, Matthew responded. "Yes, Dan, if you can. Do you have something handy to write on?"

Dan replied, "Yes sir. I'm going to put you down for a moment, okay?" He rummaged around in his desk drawer and pulled out two sheets of paper (an extravagance his boss would frown on) and a pen. Then, knowing he couldn't hold the handset and write too, he placed it close by and said, "Go ahead, sir. I'm ready to take notes."

As Matthew explained the situation with the outlaw, Billy Drake, aka William Darcy and asked for extra security for Chance, Dickie and Abner as they spirited a strongbox filled with gold and banknotes out of Seattle, (Matthew withheld the fact that the gold was fake as well as the notes, for Sweetie's sake) an ancient Chinese man named Qin Dow pushed a broom around the sheriff's office.

He and a number of other Chinese men and women had been hired by the Seattle Police Department in a charitable effort to help the Orientals hosted by the Presbyterian Church. It was true that there were many downtrodden and starving Celestials in the city, and the more prominent religious leaders in the city had called upon the bigger establishments like City Hall, the Police Departments, and hospitals to hire workers at a low but ultimately fair wage.

The arrangement seemed to be working, at least enough

to assuage the collective religious conscience. Most of the workers were punctual, hard-working and silent. The Sheriff's department had never been so clean and old Dow was as silent as a ghost.

He was not, however, a ghost. Qin Dow had one allegiance, and that was to the Tong...the last vestige of honor and security from the homeland he had left so long ago. There were many factions within the city, but happily, these factions worked together to form a whole; unlike the Tong in San Francisco, where warring factions had gone at each other's throats over power and money, and ultimately destroyed itself.

The new telephone on Davis' desk loudly bleated Matthew's words and Dow listened intently. He spoke passable English and understood it well, although he pretended not to. It was safer that way, he thought, for if one of the white apes knew he understood their words, they would either recruit him to do their bidding, or they would not speak openly around him, and that would not do at all.

Qin Dow was a runner for the Chinatown Tong and his assistance to the Tong leaders kept food in his wife and family's bellies and kept him safe from harm. Unbeknownst to the white men and women who had hired him to work for the police department, he was a wealthy man. Oh, maybe not rich like many of the citizens of Knob Hill, but he and his kin lived in a modest but adequate apartment, had plenty of food and clothes on their backs, and the best Chinatown had to offer.

Many times over the last nine months, since he'd been hired by the police to clean their offices, Dow had been able to gather intelligence that was advantageous to the Tong. Once, he'd been able to foil an arrest of Tong members who ran a brothel just outside of Chinatown. The whore house proprietors and all the girls, alerted to the fact that the police were coming to shut them down, disappeared overnight. He had been given one hundred dollars as a reward for that intel.

A couple of months ago, he had also heard a bunch of policemen talking about a drug sting that was to take place in two days' time down at the docks. His intelligence had thwarted that effort, and he'd received even more money, and a personal handshake from his boss, Sammy Chen.

Now, hearing that a strongbox filled with gold and banknotes was about to disappear into the wastelands of Eastern Washington, he almost smiled. Being very good at his job, however, he merely stooped, stone-faced, to sweep dirt and dust into a dustbin, stood back up and headed toward the indoor privy to combat the white ape's waste.

***

A few miles away, stored in the very back of Seattle First Bank, a certain strongbox hissed alarmingly. No one was around to hear the abrupt noise, but the three baby rattlers that were born inside of the crate while on route from California to Seattle surged and hissed in annoyance.

Their mother, which had wriggled into the dark, dusty receptacle to bear her progeny, expired from the weight of the heavy sack of gold-colored lead coins placed in the box, but not before the hatchlings were born and now, they needed to get out fast, before they expired as well.

They did not know that death awaited their eventual escape, and that day would arrive soon. In three days, to be exact. They only knew that the poison inside of them bubbled and writhed like a living thing, and that ridding themselves of that built-up toxicity was paramount.

Someone would soon feel that poisonous fire, and his death would set into motion a hellish storm of blame, re-crimination and revenge.

28

Dow left his workplace and ran towards Chinatown. He was excited and, perhaps a little scared. This would be the first time he broke the chain of command. It wasn't because his boss, Sammy Chen, wasn't a good man. It was because the take would be huge (if that Matthew fellow could be believed), and the police would be directly involved in the take down.

He had sat in on many Tong meetings and been told, over and over again, that anything to do with policemen in Seattle should go directly to the Tong leaders; not to their lieutenants, who were known to be ambitious and corrupt.

Still, he thought as he bustled to a Chinese restaurant just outside of the barred gates of Chinatown, in order to appease the big players in Seattle's Tong hierarchy, he would probably incur the wrath of his own boss, Sammy Chen.

Shrugging mentally, he stepped inside a smoke-filled café and bowed to the restaurant's manager, a lean, dour faced man named An Mi Lin, or Andy. He asked the much taller man if the Tong leadership would receive his call and confided the fact that his newest intelligence involved copious amounts of gold.

Andy glared and made a show of deciding if such a lowly person such as himself was worth bothering the bosses over, and then turned and walked to the back where a number of black suited men sat at a long table, sipping tea. One of the men peered past Andy's lean frame, and Lee saw him nod in affirmation.

Andy made his way back to where Dow stood and said, "You better not be wasting his time…"

Dow answered, "I am not, and you would do well to remember that."

Surprised at the runner's boldness and impressed by his confidence, Andy bowed slightly and used his hand in a sweeping gesture to lead the way to the back of the café. Dow followed, and hoped the sudden perspiration dampening his armpits did not show. Showing fear or weakness to the Tong leadership was a bad idea.

Also, he admonished himself, *I may be getting older and arthritis might gnaw at my hands and feet, but my ears work just fine, and that Matthew person said there was a fortune in the strongbox for the taking! This news may just elevate me from a humble runner to lieutenant!*

As he approached the long table, Dow saw that there were two prominent Tong leaders sitting at the far end. Several *boo how doy*, or paid soldiers filled the other seats, along with a number of delectable Asian party girls, who sat together in a gaggle smoking cigarettes and trying hard not to look bored.

"Qin Dow!" one of the leaders exclaimed brightly. "You have returned to us again. How may we be of service?" Which, Dow knew, was code for, *you better not be wasting our time, or your service will no longer be tolerated.*

Feeling sweat prickle his chest and upper back, Dow answered, "Sirs, if you please, I have new intelligence for you. Very valuable intel, but..." he cast his eyes about nervously. "humbly, and I am very sorry, there are too many ears here. This is delicate, and very secret information."

As expected, his words caused one of the leaders and most of the soldiers to scowl in anger. The girls perked up as well, looking fully engaged and interested, but the big boss, known as Lucky, sat up straight and said, "That is fine, Dow." He tossed his napkin down, adding, "Please, follow me into the back. We will enjoy more privacy there."

Dow followed the older man through a door leading to a long bar, soft lights and some poker tables and beyond, into a private office. As he passed the table, though, he couldn't help but notice how affronted the other Tong leader and the soldiers remained. The girls suddenly decided to get to work and many of them clambered onto the men's laps, writhing sensuously and tonguing the soldiers' cheeks and ears.

Dow wondered if he would even make it out of this café alive but sighed knowing that if his goose was finally cooked, he would go down trying with his last breath to help his beloved Tong, warts and all.

Once seated in the back room, Dow felt his nervousness fall away and he eagerly told Mr. Lucky everything he'd heard that afternoon; about the strongbox filled with gold and banknotes, the Spokane deputies who were scheduled to ferry said fortune to the Spokane area and how this was all designed to bring down an outlaw named Billy Drake. He admitted, he'd also heard the name Matthew Wilcox and another name, Sweetie Mack.

Mr. Lucky frowned thoughtfully and asked, "Did you say that the Seattle police department will be involved in this scheme?"

Dow shook his head. "Well, the detective said he would try to bring some police in to help the Spokane County deputies on their way back to Spokane City. It was a one-sided discussion, honorable sir, but I gathered that those men expect to be robbed by that Billy Drake man. They plan on it!"

"Well, well, well," Lucky mused. This information was indeed valuable and worthy of his own boss' knowledge and approval. The Seattle Tong were still smarting financially. When they'd fled California, they were lucky to get away with their skins still intact, much less with the riches that had once made them so strong. Although they had recovered some of their previous wealth, a large amount of gold would not go unappreciated.

He grinned, and Dow released a large breath he did not know he'd been holding. His intelligence was being well received, and maybe now he would be rewarded with a cash bonus or even a promotion!

Lucky saw the thoughts that ran across the runner's face like golden carp under shallow water. *This particular rat,* he thought, *has had his nose in too many private places, and now he knows far too much. It's time for him to join his fellow rats down by the docks.*

Masking his thoughts, though, he stood up, stepped behind the runner and opened the door to the hallway outside. "Please bring our friend, Qin Dow a nice pot of tea, and some noodles. He has earned it..." he said to an unknown person standing guard outside the door.

Relaxing, Dow sat back in his chair, and heaved a sigh of relief. Then, he heard Mr. Lucky say, "Lee, please enjoy our hospitality. I must leave you now and go to my boss with your news. Goodbye."

Lucky closed the door behind him as he left, and Dow felt a stir of hunger in his belly. He had not eaten all day, although the white apes he worked for constantly offered him their nasty American food. Knowing how good the food here was, he smiled in anticipation of the upcoming feast.

Many minutes passed, and then many more, until Dow began to wonder if Mr. Lucky's food order had been forgotten. He was about to stand up and take his leave, when the door finally opened. But, instead of the inviting aroma of tea and noodles, he smelled musk and sweat and heard the heavy rasp of steel on steel.

Heart stuttering in his chest, Dow ran to the far wall and blurted, "What! What have I done to deserve this?"

An old, old man grinned, and Dow felt a trickle of urine run down his pant leg. This man was a 'High binder', and carried a ceremonial sword in one hand, and a hatchet in the other. The man's long, white queue was bound tight to the top of his head, and Dow understood this was one of the Seattle Tong's high executioners.

He had only a moment to feel the honor of being dispatched by one of China's top assassins, before the man's sword lopped his head off in one stroke.

Later, Dow's dismembered body fell into a rubbish heap by one of Seattle's docks and his head made its way home, to serve as a warning to other men in Chinatown who strove to emulate their betters.

29

Matthew hung up the phone and tried to think of any other loose ends in their scheme to end Billy Drake's reign of terror in Chelan County. Even the most well-laid plans had pit falls and hazards, and a stray bullet could catch up to anyone, whether they be good or bad. But, he mused, those happenstances were God's will.

Matthew was no longer sure if God really existed, or if His plans on earth meant good or ill, or anything *at all* to the people He'd created. Matthew had seen too much evil in his time on earth to think that God rewarded only the just. In his own personal experience, some of the worst men and women on the planet seemed to benefit while other, more noble folks suffered. Still, his beloved wife, Iris, believed deeply in her Lord. In her honor, Matthew tried to believe as well.

It doesn't hurt to hedge one's bets, though, he thought. Getting the Seattle police involved not only wrapped his son and friends in another blanket of security, it brought in more eye-witness lawmen to help bring Billy Drake down. He had read a passage some time ago that went something like; God helps those who help themselves. Well, that's me for sure.

Chance, Dicky and Abner were leaving this afternoon by train to Seattle. If things went as planned, they would bring Sweetie's strong box back home by coach tomorrow, where hopefully many Eastern Washington lawmen would nab the would-be thieves and force them to turn State's evidence against Drake and his gang.

Hearing a shout of laughter outside, he got up from behind his desk and walked to window to see what was going on. His mouth dropped open a little as he watched Chance and Sweetie engaging in a round of swordplay down by the front corral.

Chance had always been an outstanding swordsman. Matthew had introduced his son to fencing when he was still just a boy, and he'd grown to excel in the fighting sport while in the Army. Chance had continued in the art and still practiced religiously at least three times a week.

Watching the mock dual taking place on the grounds in front of the corral, Matthew was astonished to see that Sweetie was easily keeping pace with the younger man, and actually out-scoring him on a few finer points. Chance's face was beet-red with effort, but the young woman barely seemed winded.

Grinning, Matthew picked up his hat, placed it on his head and ran downstairs to watch the show.

***

Even as Chance was having his 'sword-fighting' butt handed to him by a woman on a fine morning in Granville, Washington, Kevin Woolsey and Pete Meadows were boarding a Seattle-bound train in Wenatchee, and Darcy's two minor lieutenants, Carmichael and Hampsted were riding in an old wagon toward the city of Spokane and west to, hopefully, be in place for the heist which should take place the next day.

Denny was happily munching on a pork rind, even though the heavy salt cure puckered his mouth and chapped his lips. He was thinking about his promised share of the dough onboard that fast-approaching stagecoach. He was also thinking about taking that share and fleeing the area. He would regret leaving his boss behind, but he was sick and tired of all the hungry mouths he was expected to keep full.

He had never loved the woman he'd married, and although his daughters were cute enough when they were first born, he hated seeing their pinched, starving faces and the hollow-eyed stares of fear and disappointment they cast his way whenever he entered the room.

Yes! he thought, *why go back to them at all? Once this job is done, I'll go to Darcy's mansion, pick up my cut and skedaddle on out of town!* He had cousins in Oregon, after all, and at one time, they'd been close. Maybe he'd head on over to Portland and see what life was like there.

As Denny contemplated his selfish but blissful reward, Roger stared at the back of his partner's big red neck and wondered if he should just run a knife around it now and get it over with. God knew, his fingers itched to do it, but he reckoned he'd need the stupid lout's help when it came time to rob the coach.

He had *no* intention, however, of grabbing the dough and meekly handing it over to those dirty dogs, Woolsey and Meadows. He wanted that fortune for himself, because he was absolutely convinced that Darcy was going down for the count, which would mean, of course, that he would go down with him. Plus, he had a strong feeling of foreboding; as though a dark, dangerous cloud, swift and resolute was chasing him down, threatening an otherwise beautiful June morning with invisible menace.

Carmichael pulled his mount up short and pointed down at a rocky hollow spotted with quaking aspens and willow switches. A small, blue creek wound its way through the trees and boulders. Even as Roger dwelled in his own violent daydreams, he felt a sense of cool calm emanating from that deep creek, and he licked dry lips. "What is it, Denny?"

"Whal, I was thinking we're early, and I figure we got the drop on 'em, so how's about heading down yonder and resting easy for a while?" he grinned and Hampsted shuddered with disgust. The man's whole face was smeared with pork tallow, and thick bits of sinew showed between Denny's jagged, buck teeth. "Whadya say, Hampsted? I got a broken-down pole in my saddlebags, and that looks like a good place to dig up some craw daddies."

Yes, Roger thought. *It's also a good, deep watering hole to bury your miserable carcass after you help me rob that coach!* He kept his thoughts to himself, but nodded curtly, to Carmichael's delight.

Whooping, Carmichael snapped the reins over their horse's backs and brought them up to a canter, sending the wagon jogging and swaying over the bouldered hillside. "Slow down, dammit!" Hampsted shouted, but Carmichael just grinned and snapped the reins again.

Praying the wagon would not tumble over a headlong cliff before they reached the creek, Roger thought dismal thoughts about fools and their many assorted ends...and how the dang fool next to him was about to come to his own end – and right soon.

30

Later that night, an impromptu parade took place near Chinatown. The police were alerted to their presence, but since the crowd was docile there was no need to bring in reinforcements, or so they thought.

The parade goers were actually rather somber, which caused the five police officers in attendance to scratch their heads. *These celestials,* they thought, *are as inexplicable as the stars, and just as remote.* Usually, they raucously celebrated their precious oriental holidays; the Chinese New Year (Spring Festival) or the Lantern Festival, but that holiday occurred on the 15th of January, which was long past. The police department was aware of those and prepared. But, once in a while, an event would occur that had no discernable public meaning.

Sometimes, the officers knew, the Chinese people were attending a funeral, or the birth of an important baby, or partaking in a celebration of an auspicious wedding. Still, those almost always occurred in the light of day- not like now, at 2:30 at night.

Still, the people were quiet, but for a couple of dark-clad characters who tapped drums at the front and back of the line. Other than that, they refrained from disturbing the peace, so the Seattle officers stood back and let the procession move past unmolested.

Unbeknownst to the policemen, there were many boo how doy (paid soldiers) in attendance. That knowledge would have galvanized the police into action because the oriental fighters were well-known and feared throughout the community. They would also have been horrified to learn that at least three highly paid Chinese assassins were intermingled with the crowd.

But the officers remained blissfully ignorant as five men, dressed in black, peeled away from the back of the parade and made their stealthy way down an alleyway that skirted the Seattle First Bank. As if on cue, the rearmost drummer started pounding his drum harder and faster.

As the watching officers exchanged glances and wondered whether or not to stop the louder drummer, two of the five Tong soldiers worked rapidly to remove a metal-meshed window covering from the back of the bank. A couple of pry-bars made short work of the secured window and, as the drumbeats beat a tattoo in the night, the boo how doy flowed through the window like smoke and moved into the bank's warehouse.

There were a number of strongboxes stored on the shelves, but one box caught their immediate attention. It was clean for one thing and standing out because most of the other boxes were covered in a thick layer of dust. In addition, the box was engraved with the initials, SM. After a quick, whispered consultation with one of the soldiers that spoke fluent English, the thieves determined that the engraved letters probably stood for Sweetie Mack.

Satisfied that they had found the prize, the soldiers picked up the box and flowed back out the window. The parade had passed by now, and the sound of drumbeats were fading away into the night. It had not taken them long to steal the box, but time was of the essence now, if they wanted to keep the Tong's culpability a secret.

They placed the heavy box into a beautiful burgundy-colored buggy, and then the Tong lieutenant whispered to two of the youngest members to re-attach the metal mesh to the window and ordered the other soldiers to disperse and make themselves invisible for the rest of the night.

Then, even before the drumbeats of the departing parade had faded completely away, the buggy sped toward the Tong leadership's official headquarters; a beautiful mansion on Nob Hill.

It was 3:15 in the morning.

✸✸✸

The snakes inside the strongbox had fallen into a state of hibernation in an attempt to stave off death. Snakes were capable of hibernating for long periods of time, especially northern rattlers, which were forced into deep holes during times of snow and cold temperatures.

Still, most holes in the ground played host to a variety of food sources, like bugs and rodents, roots and seeping water. These baby snakes were starving to death, and too dazed to move their rattles.

So, except for one weak buzz, which was masked by the sound of the horses' hooves on the cobblestoned streets, the snakes moved through the night to emerge, suddenly, into a well-lit office in the home of the Seattle Tong's most honorable leader, Zhang Wei.

31

Chance, Dicky and Abner had arrived in Seattle in the wee hours of morning thanks to two breakdowns of the westbound train. Both breakdowns called for "All hands, on deck". The first was a stretch of track that had been disturbed close to the Cascade Mountain range.

Every able-bodied man was asked to help re-lay the tracks, which was nerve-wracking as the tracks ran along a scree slick patch of earth with a steep incline on one side of the train and an even steeper drop-off into an abyss on the other.

They were finally on their way about two hours later and chugging merrily along when the train slowed again, this time at a scheduled stop for additional wood to power the steam engines. All would have been well, but for the fact that the cut-up cordwood was not in the hopper that hovered above the train, but scattered on the ground, mired in spring snow and mud.

It took another hour and a half to manually load wood onto the train, and then, finally, the locomotive made its way over the mountains summit, and ran downhill into the city of Seattle. The trip should have taken approximately ten hours, but the breakdowns pushed their arrival time back by four and a half hours.

Worn to the quick, all three men made their weary way into a hotel and slept like dead men until 11:30 the next morning. Waking up with a start, Dicky sprang out of bed and shook his friends awake. "Hey! Abner, Chance, wake up, we're late!"

Abner grunted and Chance sat up in bed with a groan. He had worked hard last night, but not *that* hard! Grimacing, he knew that the impromptu sword practice yesterday had taxed muscles he'd forgotten he had, and he was paying now for his arrogance. *But, good God!* he thought. That woman could really fence – better than he did, for sure, but also just as well as his father, and certainly better than his sword master in the Army!

Grinning at the thought, he stood up and said, "What time is it, anyway? Feels like I just closed my eyes."

Dicky nodded. "For me too, but it's almost noon! We gotta get to the bank."

"Noon! Are you kidding me?" Chance gasped. "Sheesh, Pa will be pissed at us for being slug-a-beds...let's not tell him, okay?"

Dicky shrugged. "As long as we make it well out of town by this evening with that box, there's no need to tell Matthew we slept in. We're only about three hours off schedule. But let's make it quick!"

The men dressed quickly and made their way to Seattle First Bank, which to Dicky's eyes looked to be busy with police...too busy. Heart sinking, he turned to his friends and said, "Oh, oh. Looks like there might have been a hold-up here."

Chance frowned and agreed, "Yeah, looks like something has happened. Let's go see."

Making their way inside, Dicky flashing his badge the whole way, they walked up to one of the tellers and asked, "Hello! We're here to pick up a strongbox. Can you help us?"

The teller, a young man with pimples and a worried expression answered, "A strongbox, you say?" Blushing nervously, he gulped and said, "You better go and talk to the bank manager. He's just over there, talking to that policeman."

Feeling a chill of alarm, Chance led the way and approached a rotund, black-suited man who was gesturing wildly, his cheeks red with wrath. "But," he sputtered. "you said that the cops would keep an eye out for bandits! Now, my bank has to stand surety against the contents of that box, and I don't think we have enough insurance to cover it. Honestly, we should sue you and your department!"

The police officer's face turned red, and he opened his mouth for a sharp reply when Chance interrupted. "Excuse me, but my name is Chance Wilcox." Turning slightly toward his companions, he added, "And, this is Deputy Dick McNulty, and Abner Smalley. We've come here to fetch a strongbox. Here's the lading slip…"

He handed the paper to the bank manager, who sucked a breath in through clenched teeth. Chance knew what the man was going to say, but felt rage diffuse his cheeks before he even heard the banker's words.

"Yes, um…er," the older man stuttered. "My name is Clarence Townsend, the manager of this bank and… er, that particular box seems to have gone missing." Seeing the cold-eyed stare (much like his father's) leveled at him by the young man, he added, "But, it's not our fault! I blame the police department. We pay good money for security around here, and still, someone managed to break in here last night, and they got off with your strongbox!"

The police officer protested, and as the two men argued, Chance turned to Dicky and whispered, "Well, what do we do now?"

The older man shrugged and said, "We need to call your dad but first, let's see if the police have any clue about what happened."

Turning to the red-faced police officer, Dicky flashed his star and said, "Excuse me, but do you men have any idea who the culprits might be?"

As though relieved to talk to a reasonable, star-bearing human being instead of the furious little banker, he answered, "No clue, sir. We have gone over the area with a fine-toothed comb and can find no evidence of who did the deed."

Dicky smiled, and asked, "I'm one of the police officers

charged with bringing that box back to the Spokane area. As such, would you permit me to have a look at the scene?"

Looking somewhat put-out, but cowed by the mornings events, the policeman shrugged and said, "Sure, why not? You won't find anything, though. Me and my men have searched the whole area but the only thing we found was a little brick mortar outside in the alley by a barred window. We're thinking that window was how they broke in. So, follow me, please."

Then, turning to the banker, the officer snapped, "And *you* had better put in a phone call to the police commissioner if you wish to file suit. I am done with your abuse!"

With those words, the man spun on his heels and marched toward the back of the bank and through a series of doors. Finally, they arrived at a heavy metal door which opened onto a large, dusty storeroom. There were two barred windows at the back of the room and enough sunlight streamed through the bars to show a million motes of dust which surged and drifted lazily on the disturbed air like ghosts.

Walking toward a set of shelves, Chance saw a bare, dust-free rectangle on the top shelf which had, apparently, hosted Sweetie's missing strongbox. Fury filled his heart. The box was gone, for sure, and he had no idea how to fetch it back.

Looking at Dicky, he noticed the deputy was staring at the floor. "Do you see anything?" he asked.

Unfortunately, Dicky shook his head. "No, but what I *am*

seeing amazes me…" he pursed his mouth in concentration.

"What? What are you seeing?" Abner asked.

"Well, someone took the time to sweep the floor before they left. See?"

Abner and Chance both studied the floor and, indeed, they saw nothing but broom marks leading from where they stood back toward the right-hand window.

"Now, what kind of crook brings a broom along on a heist?" Dicky wondered aloud.

"The very good and sneaky kind of crook, I reckon," the policeman answered.

32

As Chance spent time and money to place a long-distance call to his father on the other side of the state, Kevin Woolsey and Pete Meadows made their way by buggy to their boss' 5th Street apartment in Seattle. The three of them had come by locomotive to Seattle the day before, but while Pete and Kevin rode in the passenger carriage, Drake traveled in a rented caboose, filled with fine furnishing, a small bar and a private sleeping-berth.

Upon arriving in the city, Woolsey and Meadows left the station on their own and some minutes later, Drake took a private carriage to his small but opulent apartment. He was waiting impatiently for the box' arrival and glancing at his pocket watch when he heard a knock on the front door.

He let his private butler answer the door and sat in his armchair rehearsing the dressing-down he planned on giving his lieutenants when they finally made an appearance. The words died on his lips, however, when Pete barged in and said, "The box is gone!"

Drake scowled and barked, "Say what? What do you mean it's gone?"

Pete and Kevin both glared in return, and Kevin insisted, "What Pete says is true, sir. The whole bank is buzzing about it! Seems some crook, or crooks, busted through a back window of the bank last night, and made off with the loot."

Drake was stunned. Who knew about the box, besides the owners of it and he and his top lieutenants? Well, besides his minions, Roger, Denny, Andrew Forsythe and the Black Cat but they had no clue of Billy's plans... did they? Going for the most obvious conclusion, he asked, "Was it the owners of the Lucky Lady? Did they come in early and grab it?"

Both men shook their heads, and Pete said, "No sir, we don't think so. See, we were standing in the bank lobby, along with the rest of the bank tellers and customers when the cops showed up. We were standing toward the back, but we saw a group of men, including a Spokane County deputy, question the bank manager about the box. They had been sent, apparently, to ferry the strongbox back to Spokane. They looked pretty shook-up about it and just as confused as we were, So, no. Unless this was some sort of double-blind perpetrated by the Luck Lady owners, the money has disappeared; from all of us!"

Pete stopped talking abruptly. He was not one to give a speech or explain himself, but he'd seen the evil anger moving behind Billy's eyes like a coiled-up snake ready to strike and wanted no part of his boss' wrath. That money up and walking off was not his fault, nor Kevin's. Someone had gotten the drop on all concerned and he did not want to shoulder the blame.

Billy Drake understood Pete's words then and slumped back in his fine leather chair. *Is the game up, then?* he wondered. *Or, has Sammy Chen betrayed me? Either way, I'm doomed to failure. If Chen has alerted the Tong to the wealth in that box, then the fortune is lost to me and I will not even think about stealing it back.*

Rage filled his heart then. Suddenly, it all seemed so clear. He had told his old friend, Sammy, about the fortune in that box, but instead of taking a generous portion of the money for himself, Chen had done the "honorable" thing and informed his beloved Tong, effectively hanging Billy out to dry!

Seeing the look of rage on Billy's face, Kevin and Pete took an unconscious step back and waited for the ax to fall. But they were surprised when Billy merely shook his head and murmured, "Well, the gig is over for us, boys. The only thing I can think is that Sammy betrayed my trust to the Tong. And, that means our hands are tied."

He sighed, and for the first time Pete couldn't help but notice the etch of time on his boss' face. He seemed diminished, suddenly, and out of his depth.

Sensing Peter's regard, Billy sat up in his chair and growled, "You men don't understand the Tong. How powerful they are, and vicious with it. If we even attempt to steal that box back, our heads will depart our bodies and we'll be nothing more than fodder for Chinese pigs!"

He stood up in agitation and continued. "Now, I want you two to head back home and lay low for a while. I'll follow you back soon, but I need to make a couple of phone calls first and go to see someone. I'll head back home tomorrow."

He smiled then. "And once I do get back, we'll pay a visit to the Black Cat and his uncle, Andrew Forsythe. Maybe they know something that we don't."

✳✳✳

At 1:30 that same afternoon, Zhang Wei finished his bath, and rose from the jasmine scented water with a smile. Studying his long, pointed fingernails, he nodded in satisfaction. His youngest courtesan was raw and somewhat uncouth, but she had made a fine study of manicure, and had done him proud this morning.

At sixty-two-years-old, Zhang Wei was still a strong man and handsome. That strength and fortitude of character was vital for a leader of the Tong in Seattle, and never more so than today. Many high-ranking Lieutenants and *boo how doy* would be coming by today to watch the opening of the stolen strongbox, and to behold the riches that had just fallen into their laps.

Now, Zhang Wei thought, *finally, the Seattle-based*

Tong will enjoy the wealth we once took for granted in San Francisco.

He heard the voice of his eldest son in the adjoining room and snapped at the many women in the room to hurry their chore of helping him dress. They jumped into action, and a few minutes later, Zhang emerged from the bathroom resplendent in black trousers, a white dress shirt and a long, silk robe.

Looking at his son, who sat by the door on a long divan, he asked, "Have they arrived yet?"

The young man, who was named after his father, answered, "Yes, father. Most are seated in the dining room now, waiting on your arrival."

Zhang nodded, and thought, *as they should always be made to await the arrival of their betters.* Out loud, he said, "Well, let's not keep them waiting any longer. This is a big day – for all of us! Maybe now, we shall have just as much power and influence in this city as the Yakuza."

His son bowed slightly and fell behind his father as they made their way down the curved staircase, and further, into the huge dining room. As expected, almost all of the high-ranking Tong members and their minions sat at the long table with hushed looks of expectation on their faces.

Zhang clapped his hands, and said, "As many of you already know, some of my *boo how doy* stole a strongbox last night from the Seattle First bank. This box," he gestured at the shabby-looking strongbox, "contains a veritable fortune in gold and banknotes. Now, my good friends," he exclaimed, "the Tong will be rich and more powerful than ever!"

A whisper of excitement rippled around the room and every man there strained forward to view the contents of the box as Zhang's son and two of their most trusted *boo how doy* bent down with prybars to loosen the lid.

The lid gave way with a rusty screech, and suddenly a loud, angry buzz filled the air and Zhang's son fell back with a strangled cry. A collective gasp filled the air as they saw the young man fall to the floor with three wriggling rattlesnakes attached to his face.

It took only seconds for the Chinese soldiers to dispatch the snakes, but the rattlers' poison was already racing through the boy's bloodstream. Zhang watched, stricken and horrified as his son's face turned bright red and then white. The young man's throat swelled to three times its usual size, and his tongue protruded from black descended lips.

Two of Zhang's medicine men ran into the room to lend assistance, but one of them, the oldest and best medicine man in Chinatown, stood back and shook his head. Turning to Zhang Wei, he murmured, "I am so very sorry, exalted leader, but your boy is already dead."

As the toughest Chinese gangster in all of Seattle watched the spark of life shrivel and flee from his son's eyes, and saw the horror on his soldiers' faces, his heart filled with wrath.

Then, with a mumbled curse, Zhang Wei fainted, and his head came to rest on the chest of his first-born son.

33

Matthew hung up the phone and sat staring at the far wall of his office. *Dammit!* he thought. All that work and jock-eying to find actual lawmen to legitimize Drake's take down and, just like that, Sweetie's strongbox had disappeared into thin air!

He knew there was no way he, or anyone he knew, would be able to track the phony fortune down and he hardly saw the point of even trying. The thieves would soon find out that they had wasted their time and energy on gold-plated lead, and as soon as they tried to cash in on the banknotes, they would also know they were fake as well.

Serves them right! he thought. Of course, Matthew had no way of knowing that a rattlesnake had slithered its way into the wood-rotted box and were now as dead as door-nails, or the fact that the Tong leader, Zhang Wei's son had died from the snakes' venom. Had Matthew known, he would not be half-smirking at the thieves' failure now.

Still... he sighed. Sweetie's plans had just come to an

abrupt halt, and he needed to go down and tell her about it. He stood up and walked over to the window, looking down into the yard. *No Sweetie; she must be inside the house.*

Leaving his office, Matthew took the staircase down and saw Sweetie curled up at a window seat in the parlor, reading a book. Hearing his footsteps, she placed a bookmark in the novel and smiled up at him. Seeing the look on his face, she frowned and asked, "Hi, Matthew. What's up?"

Matthew went to the sideboard and grabbed two whiskey tumblers. "Care to join me?"

Looking from his eyes to the bottle of whiskey in his hands, she answered, "Sure…I guess. Matthew, what's going on?"

Matthew poured two neat whiskeys and after handing her a drink, sat down and said, "The strongbox was robbed from the bank last night, Sweetie."

Sweetie's whiskey tumbler paused in mid-air as Matthew's words hit her like a bullet to the head. Her eyes grew wide, and she said, "What? How! Who did it, do you know?"

Matthew shook his head. "No, I don't know, and neither do the cops. Chance, Roy and Abner walked into the bank this morning to fetch it, and everyone is left scratching their heads. Seems like that box was the only thing the crooks wanted, though, as everything else was left untouched."

Sick at heart, Sweetie set her drink down and sprang up off the window seat with a huff of disgust. "God! Matthew, how do you think the thieves found out about it? Was it Drake?"

Watching the lovely young woman pacing back and forth like a caged lion, Matthew sighed. He had known all along that there were *A Lot* of moving parts in their scheme. Too many, really. Just about everyone in Sweetie's outfit were aware of the sting, and so were a couple of side-players like Andrew Forsythe and Tommy 'The Black Cat' Kirwin. In addition, they had made sure that Billy Drake knew about the fortune traveling overland to the Spokane area.

Anyone could have blabbed about the fortune in that strongbox; whether willingly or not. *Hell,* he mused, *it could even have been one of my guys!*

He trusted his men, of course. His son, Dicky and Abner he trusted with his life. But even they weren't perfect… they could have shared some of the sting's details with law-men out of Spokane county, or discussed the situation with Steve Mercer, who went on to share the particulars with an unknown hostile player.

He thought about his own culpability…did the Seattle detective, Dan Davis spill the beans somehow while trying to get permission to monitor the situation on his end? Unfortunately, the more he thought about it, the surer he became that he, himself, had maybe made a crucial mistake.

He asked Sweetie, "Just wondering, how many people in your outfit knew that the strongbox would be stashed away in the bank's warehouse?"

Sweetie's eyes flashed. "Sir, my own trusted advisors, Edwin Trask, Steven Mercer, and Randall Winters all knew that was where the box would be shipped to from California." Eyes narrowing, she added, "I really hope you're not accusing them of the theft? They all knew that the box's contents were nothing but rubbish!"

Matthew held up his hands in surrender. "No! I am not accusing them of anything." His voice had risen in agitation, but he took a deep breath and said, "Actually, I wonder if *I* am not responsible!" He glared and swallowed the rest of his drink in one burning gulp.

Sweetie asked, "How so, Matthew?"

He shook his head. "It's just that I made a phone call to an old acquaintance of mine, Detective Dan Davis, in Seattle a couple of days ago. I was seeking extra security but maybe, somehow, he let word slip that there was a fortune to be guarded in the bank's warehouse section…but, honestly, the leak could have come from anywhere or anyone."

Sweetie sat back down with a sigh. "You're right. Still, my best plans to bring Billy down just went poof! What am I going to do now?"

***

It was a beautiful early summer afternoon with clear, blue skies and fat, billowy clouds that sailed across the firmament like galleons at sea.

Denny was having the time of his life catching fish, and despite the man's low character, Roger Hampsted had to admit Denny was a pretty good fish tickler. They had stuffed themselves on crawdaddies last night and now four trout, five bass, and a long, eel-looking thing with jagged teeth drifted on a leaded line in the cool river water.

Roger knew that the coach they were supposed to rob wasn't due until later on today and he was allowing himself to rest and relax. Relaxation was not a normal component of his character; but this little hollow, with its tinkling brook and green, lacy willow branches drifting around them like a bride's veil had dulled his defenses and he felt his eyelids lower and close as the sun warmed his face.

In spite of the day's cheerful beauty, Roger's dreams were filled with anxious shadows and dreadful, darting fingers of fear. He had sunk deeply into slumber and didn't hear the quiet footfalls approaching him and his partner from behind, but he did rouse to Denny's nasal shout of hello.

Prying his eyelids open, he stared, dazzled, into two man-shaped figures, looming like gargoyles out of the sage brush and tumbleweeds. "Howdy, boys!" Denny gushed. "Whatchu doing here?"

"Shut up, Denny," Roger hissed and fingered the grip of his pistol which lay, cockeyed, in the dust at his right hip. He eyed the men's silhouettes and saw that; indeed, they were Darcy's men. Young men, and raw, but they were a part of his own gang and for a moment, his grip on the gun's holster loosened.

But then, as his eyes adjusted to the buttery light, he saw that both men held their pistols at the ready. Pulling his gun with lightning-fast speed, he barked, "Stow those pistols, fellas, or I'll put you down where you stand!"

Denny exclaimed, "Hey! Hey, now Roger, let's not be hasty..." but an ear-shattering roar rippled through the air, and a hole appeared in the middle of Denny's forehead. The man's eyes crossed in an almost comical display of surprise and then his body slammed backward into the creek.

Roger held no affection for his partner and had already planned on putting an end to Denny's miserable, wife-beating hide, but seeing him leak his life blood into the damp earth, filled his heart with both rage and fear. Without a second thought, Roger canted his pistol up at an angle and shot Denny's assassin through the heart. Blood blew out from the young man's back, spraying the little glade with a fine red mist.

Roger, still sitting on the ground, started climbing to his feet but before he could stand, the other mercenary, a kid named...Kenneth something or other, shot Roger in the belly.

Roger bent over at the waist, gagging, but managed to keep his feet under him. Even as Kenneth took aim, Roger shot again and the boy fell dead at his feet, the bullet in his neck still smoking.

Then, swaying slightly and shocked by what had just happened, he stared at the three dead men keeping him company. Knowing that Darcy had betrayed them in the most brutal way possible filled Roger's heart with loathing.

Glancing down at his belly, which burned like flames from the depths of hell, he vowed to get back at the man. But first, he needed to get rid of the bullet that had pierced him and stanch the blood that dripped his life away.

He rolled the assassins over, grabbing their guns, knives and money and then took what little coin Denny possessed. He stood looking at the wagon and decided he wanted to move at speed rather than comfort. He grabbed Denny's rifle, a shotgun, and his saddlebags and then climbed slowly, painfully, onto his own horse.

The horse snorted fearfully at the blood pumping onto its hide and then took off at a panicked gallop.

34

Zhang Wei sat behind the desk in his office, staring at the flowers festooning every flat surface in the room. He sighed. Although he was and had always been a traditionalist, his people's cultural tradition of using white for mourning was, in his opinion, terrifying and obscene.

White! he thought in despair. *The total absence of color. The visual equivalent of...nothing! This is what's happened to my son. He's been reduced to absolutely nothing. Gone, disappeared as if he'd never graced the earth at all!*

Suddenly enraged, Zhang tossed his drink at a vase of white Chrysanthemums with a shout of fury. His wife rushed into the room, saw the damage and immediately instructed the servants to bring more white flowers into the room.

Looking past her diminutive body, he saw a number of servants filling red envelopes with coins and candy; a traditional gift from the family of the deceased to honor the guests who came to the funeral. Those same guests were expected to bring cash for the grieving family members as well as Ghost money to aid the dead on their journey to the afterlife.

Thankfully, their principal geomancer had decreed that the most auspicious time for his son's funeral would not be for at least three weeks. This would mean that his son's body would need to be kept in cold storage, and a moue of distaste twisted Zhang's lips. An ignominious end, indeed, to the promise his young son had shown.

A small smiled tugged at the corner of Zhang's mouth. *However*, he mused, *that gives me some time*, he thought. *Time to exact my revenge for those who perpetrated this crime against me and my family.*

So far, he had very little information, although he did know about three of the principle players. Matthew Wilcox was one, a woman known as Sweetie Mack was another, and a crook named William Darcy had all conspired to lay him low. Within the last few day, his *boo how doy* had seized both Sammy Chen and Tommy (Lucky) Li.

Sammy had confessed that the day before his son was murdered, an old outlaw by the name of Billy Drake (aka William Darcy) had called on the telephone to offer a quarter of the box's contents to the Tong lieutenant if he would assist in relieving said box of its contents. Chan was lucky, as he was making his way to Zhang's mansion to share this news with the Tong leader, even as he was seized.

Zhang's punishment was lenient... Chan lost only the tips of his littlest fingers for speaking to the old outlaw at all and allowing himself a full dinner before making his way to the supreme leader with his information.

Chin (Lucky) Li was less fortunate. He was deprived of his right hand for killing the runner named, Qin Dow. Zhang desired nothing more than information on why three total strangers had conspired against him, and Lucky had deprived him of that much needed intelligence.

He was unmoved by Lucky's cries of protest, and as the man was carried from his office with a bloody stump that used to be his hand, he said, "You should have let me, your supreme ruler, decide that man's fate. Now, if you survive this, you will be one of our new runners. Who knows... maybe you too will be faced with a power-hungry, capricious lieutenant instead of receiving honor for the work you have done."

It never occurred to Zhang that the snakes' appearance in the box was nothing more than a quirk of fate, a cosmic accident, and that none of the suspects knew any more than he did about how the reptiles had traveled from the warm California climes to the Seattle bank.

If blame was a ribbon-wrapped package, it might be laid at the feet of Sweetie's counterfeiter – a miserly man named Higgins, who was well-known for tripping over a dollar to save a penny. In typical fashion, he had chosen to place the fake fortune in an old, cheap and half-rotted strongbox in order to save time and money rather than spring for a new box.

Higgins, had he known, would have been horrified by

the unfortunate circumstances. Had things gone as planned; it would be Sweetie, or her friends who were bit and stricken by the poisonous snakes, and he would be out of a job, his reputation ruined by his own greed.

As it was, the successful counterfeiter went about his business without a qualm as a grieving and irate Chinese gangster plotted all manner of death and destruction against Sweetie Mack, and all her friends and business partners.

✳✳✳

Chance, Dicky and Abner arrived back home the next day, and now sat talking with Matthew, Sweetie, and her partner Steven Mercer. The men were both fatigued and frustrated by what had happened to Sweetie's strongbox.

"It just vanished into thin air, Miss Sweetie," Chance said, adding, "but we have no doubt it was the principle target. There were other, way more valuable boxes stored in that warehouse; at least, according to the bank manager. So, someone dropped a dime on us. Don't have a clue who, though."

Matthew cleared his throat. "It could have been me, son."

Chance and the other men looked shocked. "You! But how?"

Matthew shook his head. "Oh, I'm not sure of anything, but I did call an old friend of mine the day before you left. Dan Davis, a Seattle detective, and a good and honorable man. I'm starting to think that, somehow, the information about that box leaked out from his office…"

Dicky interrupted, "Have you had a chance to talk to him about it?"

Matthew nodded. "Yes. He is as baffled as I am, but he did say something that got my attention. Apparently, he has a hard time – just like me – writing things down while on the telephone. He confessed to setting the earpiece down on his desk while he jotted notes about our plans and thinks now that an old Chinese man named Qin Dow might have overheard our discussion.

He went on to tell me that the man was as quiet as a mouse and often ghosted around the office, getting into places he shouldn't have been. A good worker, apparently, but nosy, and kind of sly. He has no hard evidence, mind you, but he did say that Qin Dow has not been seen nor heard from since the day we talked."

Turning to face his son, Matthew added, "That's a pretty big coincidence, right? And, Chance, you know how much I dislike coincidences."

Chance nodded, and so did Dicky. Matthew had always had an uncanny ability to unearth the truth of things, and he was well-known to be highly suspicious of anything co-incidental. He considered them just another sign along the roadmap of criminal activity to be followed up and hunted down.

"Chinese… not the Japanese Yakuza?" Steven asked.

Matthew shrugged. "Possibly, although the Tong seems more likely to me. They are becoming a force to be reckoned with in the greater Seattle area."

He sighed. "Problem with that, though… if the Tong *did* get ahold of that box, it's lost to us now. There's no way we can penetrate the Tong or negotiate with them. We might as well save them the work and slit our own throats."

Pausing for a moment, he turned back to Sweetie and said, "I'm sorry, Sweetie. If you'd like, I'd be more than happy to reimburse you for the counterfeit gold and banknotes."

Sweetie looked horrified by the thought. "No! Heavens to Betsy, I would never expect that from you. Still, it's so frustrating! Are you sure we couldn't, somehow, reason with them? They probably know by now that the contents are worthless. Maybe we could buy it back from them…"

She stopped and stared as every man there shook his head. Steven murmured, "There's no way, Sweetie. You know the Tong, from San Francisco. The Yakuza, too. We, the whites, seem like nothing more than giant talking bears to them. They think we are ignorant, brutish and cruel- nothing more than animals. If we tried to call them, or worse, went back to Seattle to confront them directly, they would shoot us down like the dogs they think we are! Face it, we lost this one."

Sweetie blew out a pent-up breath and sat back in her chair. "Yes, I know you're right. Still, it's maddening, isn't it?"

Matthew nodded. "What's even more maddening is the fact that none of the Spokane County sheriff's I've been talking to want to pursue Billy Drake. At least not right now. It's an election year and trying to take down a sitting mayor, criminal or not, is more than any one of them wants to do. They'd have to do it the "legal" way, and that would call for witnesses, (many of whom are either disappeared or dead), and the word of most of the power players in Chelan County, which we all know are in Darcy's pocket."

Sitting up straight in his chair, he added, "One thing we *can* do though, is follow you back to Wenatchee, okay? I want to talk to some of the folks affected by Drake and his henchmen. I want to sniff out some of the crimes Drake has been involved with and see if any of the lawmen down there have personal issues with their mayor. Men with badges often have clout, especially when it comes to U S Marshals."

He grinned suddenly, and his green eyes glowed. "If I can find enough evidence, I will bring the U S Marshals in as well as the Pinkertons. What do you say to that?"

35

Matthew cursed under his breath as the telephone rang. He and Chance had gotten a late start this morning and were running behind schedule to catch the 8:15 train into Spokane. Sweetie and Steven had left for Wenatchee two days earlier and Matthew meant to catch up as soon as possible. But one problem after another had served as a roadblock and he was now playing catch-up.

There would be a two-hour delay in Spokane, then he and Chance would board the train to Wenatchee. But, one more delay would blow the itinerary altogether. He paused as the telephone shrilled again and then he set his valise on the ground with a disgusted snort and turned back to re-enter his home.

He was met at the door by Abner's wife, Sarah, who said, "Matthew, it's a fellow by the name of Dan Davis. He says he has an urgent message for you."

Sighing, he glanced at Chance who was sitting his horse, pointedly studying his pocket watch. Matthew shrugged and called out, "I need to take this, son. I'll make it quick!"

Chance answered, "It had better be quick, Pa, or we'll miss the train." Then, he stepped down off his horse to pick up his father's bag and tie it on the back of his dad's saddle.

Matthew stepped inside and walked down the hall toward the kitchen where the phone sat on a table. Picking up the earpiece, he said, "Hello, Dan?"

Davis said, "Yes, Matthew, it's me. Sorry to disturb you, but we've come into some information I thought you should know about. Got a minute?"

Matthew answered, "Yeah, I've got a couple of minutes, but only that. My boy and I are trying to catch the 8:15 and we're running late. Whatcha got?"

He could hear Dan sigh on the other end of the line, and then he blurted, "It was the Tong, Matthew. We're sure of it now. Problem is our Chinese informant tells us that a bunch of snakes found their way into your friend's strongbox. Apparently, the snakes latched onto the Tong leader's son's face. He's dead, and we hear that Zhang Wei has vowed vengeance against the box's owner."

Matthew's blood turned to ice water in his veins. "Good Lord, how did he find out who owned the box?"

Davis replied, "Same way he heard about the box to begin with, I reckon. I think that little louse, Qin Dow heard every word we said and reported back to the Tong leadership. But, from what we are hearing now, Qin's spying days are over. Police found his body – minus his head – down by the docks, which is even more frustrating as now we can't bring him in for questioning. I am so sorry, Matthew. I guess loose lips really do sink ships."

Matthew felt numb but glanced over at the grandfather clock in the front parlor... 7:50. They really were going to miss the train if he didn't get a move on, and time had just become a precious commodity.

Dan spoke again. "Listen, Matthew. Take care, all right? The Tong has long arms. I know that there are Tong members in the Spokane area. So, watch your back. I'm going to call some friends we have in law-enforcement over there, and get them to watch over you, okay?"

Matthew said, "Thanks, Dan. I appreciate that. But, don't blame yourself. It wasn't your fault, or mine even. The Tong did this. I'm sorry to hear about the boy who died, but we didn't do that either. Still, I have to warn Sweetie and I've got to do it now! Take care, Dan, okay? And, thanks for the warning."

Dan Davis said goodbye and hung up. For a moment, Matthew paused and wondered if he should call the Lucky Lady right now, and risk missing the train. Then, he decided that if he and Chance arrived in Spokane on time, he would call Sweetie while they waited to board the train to Wenatchee. He couldn't see how waiting a couple of hours to inform Sweetie of the threat could hurt.

***

Sweetie, dressed again as a man, and her partner, Steven

Mercer had left for Wenatchee two days earlier. They were worried about the state of the Lucky Lady Saloon as Trask had kept in close contact with them and informed them that the place was under siege.

Almost every night, men and even woman would show up and do things to disrupt business. Sometimes, their antics did nothing more than disturb the peace, but more often they would either start a bar brawl or pull guns and knives to try and intimidate the patrons (which were fewer and fewer) or the security teams inside and out of the establishment.

It was a little after 10:00 a.m. and Sweetie sat in Trask's office looking at the books. The numbers were disheartening. They had, for a week or so, when the saloon first opened been in the "black" but were now dipping dangerously into the "red". It was the lack of paying customers, mainly, but also property damage, and the payroll for extra security that was hurting their bottom line.

Sweetie shook her head in dismay. This was a sham business, of course, designed only to bring down the old outlaw that had damaged her and her family. But, somewhere along the way, Sweetie had fallen in love with the place. As the saloon grew from scratch; with its peach and burgundy exterior, warm cozy interior, good food and fine service, she had bonded with it and felt like it was her own child.

Now, her child was being threatened at every turn. Turning away to stare out the window, she saw the Cascade Mountains in the distance and miles and miles of black dirt cropland as far as the eye could see. Although Sweetie had spent most of her life in the bay area of California, she had made no attachments there, and instead had recently turned wistful attention to this green, rich valley.

She had begun to think she could make a home here in Chelan County, with a modest saloon and the possibility of a new, perhaps wonderful life. But, as usual, Billy Drake stood in the way of her happiness.

She gritted her teeth, and the pencil in her hand snapped in her right fist. *Oh, how I wish I could snap Billy Drake's spine, just as easily as this pencil!* But, she couldn't.

The only bright light in her immediate future was the fact that Matthew and his son were scheduled to arrive this evening. She had total faith in Matthew's abilities, and his solemn vow to help her hunt down Billy Drake.

She realized that she held the man in high esteem, maybe too high. She felt as if she might even have a slight crush on him, but she knew there was nothing sexual, or even remotely romantic about her feelings. It was more like a good man – who had all the pride and nobility of her father and uncle, and none of their weaknesses – had entered her life and offered her soul a chance to heal. Finally.

She scooted her chair back to the desk and bent over the books again to see if her calculations were correct, when the telephone rang.

36

Sweetie hung up the handset and shuddered with dread. The good news... Matthew and his son, Chance were on schedule to arrive at about 3:30 this afternoon. The bad news... the Tong, *THE TONG!* were after her and her partners.

Sweetie and her friends were no strangers to the Tong. Although she and her partners had never personally run afoul of the oriental gangsters in San Francisco, the warring Chinese known as the Yakuza and the Tong had rattled the whole city with their battles over prestige, money and power.

Although most of the violence happened within the confines of Chinatown and down by the docks, a lot of it spilled over into the rest of the city, leaving whole sections of town scorched and smoking in ruin.

Apparently, the Yakuza had emerged victorious, and most of the remaining Tong members had fled north for their lives, taking up residence in Portland, Oregon and further into the Seattle, Washington area.

Thinking back on it now, Sweetie realized she had made a terrible mistake. There was no reason to believe her plans for revenge would step on any Tong toes but, if nothing else, they *were* gangsters. Stealing vast fortunes for their own use was their business model, and she had provided a huge incentive for the Tong to involve themselves in her schemes!

Somehow, word had gotten out about her fake fortune. Maybe it was Matthew – trying to attain more security for her team, or maybe it was that little Tong informant who had eavesdropped at the Seattle policestation and dropped the dime on her plans. *Shoot!* She cursed. *Shoot, shoot!*

And, as for the snakes! *Good grief,* she thought, *I just assumed that Higgins – that scamp – had used a metal strongbox to ship my goods. But why did I think so? Higgins is known as a skinflint; why would I expect him to pony up for a good, strong metal box when he could cheat and use some cheap alternative!*

She wanted to punch herself in the face. She had thought her plans were well-rounded and sound, but she knew now that they were reckless, and had caused, at least, two deaths. *By the time this is over,* she mourned, *many, many deaths could be laid at my feet!*

She swore out loud and threw her pencil across her desk. *And now I, and all my friends are at risk!*

She stood up and marched across the room to fetch her pencil when she heard a ruckus down in the dining area.

Stamping her foot in frustration, she figured her loyal agitators were back at it again, but realized that the restaurant wasn't even open yet. Still, she heard shouts of alarm, and a great knocking, as if a team of builders were pounding their hammers against the floorboards.

She ran to the door and flew out into the hallway to peer down at the bar area. To her shock, she saw a huge bull moose running amok in the restaurant. The animal was absolutely enormous, its horns so tall the tips of them could be seen running parallel with the second-story floorboards on which she stood. Sweetie couldn't help but marvel at the velvet hanging from its great, spatula-shaped antlers like moss on a Spanish oak.

Its hair was glossy and such a dark mahogany color it appeared black, under her crystal chandelier. Its gigantic muscles flexed and quivered beneath its rich pelt and its eyes rolled white in their sockets. The animal was currently snorting with wrath and scraping its right, front hoof on her fine oak floors.

Glancing past the monstrous beast she saw that someone – two someones, in fact – were standing outside the front doors, trying to hold them open so the beast could escape, but the moose either couldn't see the escape route, or was now more interested in destroying the room he'd found himself in.

She gasped as the moose charged the bar and she heard both bartenders, Marty and Ron Stine, scream and duck behind the wooden partition separating the workspace from the customer seating area. Nina Bartonelli was jabbering rapidly in Italian and, apparently, urging the two men into the back kitchen where they could all stay safe behind closed doors. Hopefully.

Sweetie ran back to her office and lifted a rifle off the back wall. She checked to make sure the gun was loaded and then marched back out into the hallway, accompanied by the sound of breaking glass. Looking down she saw that the animal had charged its own reflection in one of the four expensive mirrors hanging on the walls of the dining area.

Shoulders sagging at the cost of replacing the mirror, and also having to put an end to the magnificent beast that had found itself trapped in a human habitat, she brought the rifle up to her shoulders and took aim. The animal had stopped its rampage for the moment and stood huffing and sniffing curiously at the fresh air coming in from the open front doors.

Sweetie hesitated, and then took aim over the animal's head. BOOM! At once, the moose took three mighty bounds and leapt out onto the porch with a terrified chuff of alarm. Then it was over.

Sweetie watched as first Tommy and then Bradley appeared from where they'd been hiding behind the open doors. Tommy tipped his hat at her and said, "Good job, sir. Thanks."

She smiled slightly, gave a small salute and went back inside her office to fix her mustache. She'd sprouted a sweat during the hubbub and was worried that the hairy prosthetic was coming loose. "What in tarnation happened here?" Sweetie heard Trask say just as she walked inside her room.

Glancing in the mirror, she saw that the right-side corner of the mustache was, indeed, starting to come loose, and she applied a liberal dose of glue to her upper lip. Then, she walked back out to the hall and looking down at the three men who had just returned from the bank, said, "Mister Trask, Steven, and Edward, would you please come up here for a few minutes?"

Trask was studying the damage with disgust and looking up at her, he said, "Sure, we'll be up in just a minute, okay?"

Sweetie nodded and prepared herself to deliver even more bad news to her friends.

37

Roger Hampsted walked slowly, shakily, into his one room apartment in East Wenatchee. The room was austere and almost freakishly clean. He had spent most of his formative years in filth and squalor and had kept a promise to himself when he came of age...

Never would he allow himself to wallow in his own filth as his parents had done; choosing to drink and carouse their sorrows away, rather than elevate themselves and their children with hard work and fortitude. As far as Roger was concerned, his parents had doomed him and his siblings into a life of crime. By the time his father died, and his mother was placed in a house for the criminally insane the die was cast for their progeny.

His older sister was dead and buried; killed by her own husband in a drunken fit of rage. The other sister, little Marie, was a whore in a Seattle brothel. She was a beautiful woman and had made fairly wise decisions regarding the money she earned. Last Roger heard, Marie and another woman called Bethany Stark were living together as lovers and thriving financially.

His brother, Timothy, was long gone. Roger didn't know whether his big brother was dead and buried, or if he'd fled the country altogether. He'd been running with a vicious gang known as the Mad Hatters but had disappeared after some young upstart sheriff named Matthew Wilcox bushwhacked the gang in a little town just outside of Wenatchee.

But that was years and years ago. Roger did not grieve his brother's loss, but he did sometimes miss the shelter family could offer...at least a healthy family filled with love and support rather than hatred and fear.

He moved slowly to the kitchen table, lit a lamp and rummaged around in a paper sack filled with medical supplies he'd gotten from the local vet. Finding a small blue bottle, he picked it up and took a swallow of the laudanum contained inside. Immediately, his eyes rolled, and he could see colorful prism rainbows shining in the lantern's dim light.

Studying his room, Roger took note of his neatly made bed and all the wanted posters adorning his walls. He had made a habit of collecting wanted posters since he first saw his own image nailed to a tree outside of Portland, Oregon.

He had not been caught that time, (a train robbery) and had never seen his own likeness on a poster again. But still, he thought many of the posters were quite beautiful; men and women's images caught forever, like insects in amber, their misdeeds writ plain and simple for all to see.

Finally, Roger stood up and made his way to the bed. The vet, for an exorbitant fee, had dosed him up good and proceeded to dig a bullet out of his belly. Fortunately, the bullet had not pierced his intestines, which would have been a death sentence; but the pain was unbelievable, an intense burning ache as torn muscles tried to reknit themselves into some kind of working order.

The vet reckoned Roger would survive, as long as infection didn't set-in, but he also warned that his recovery would be slow, and not to push it if he hoped to outlive the gunshot.

Roger was strong, however, and felt he'd be back in fighting form sooner rather than later. *Which is a good thing,* he thought, as the floor and ceiling seemed to spin around his dazzled eyes.

For I have work to do...putting an end to that miserable traitor, William Darcy! He grinned even as his eyes drifted shut.

***

Chin (Lucky) Lee was not so lucky anymore. After Zhang Wei had his hand removed, he was left at home to survive or perish. Neither he nor his boss really cared.

It was a miserable time for the amputee. Both of his wives scorned him and his reduced circumstances, and only his mother kept the two women from murdering him out-right. But his mother was almost as fearsome as Zhang Wei himself, and ruled her son's home with an iron fist.

He was still in agonizing pain and racked with chills and fever when he was summoned back to the supreme leader's mansion. His mother dressed him that night and told him to hold his head up high. "Zhang Wei is like a wolf," she advised, "and like the wolf, he will sense weakness in you. Sometimes an alpha male will be driven mad with bloodlust when he senses weakness, so stand up to him with pride and honor, my son, or he will eat you alive!"

Gathering what courage he had left, Lee stepped into the carriage Zhang Wei had sent. He held his head high, and kept his stump hidden inside his coat pocket, ignoring the smirks and side-long glances of the *boo how doy* that accompanied him.

He entered Zhang Wei's office with trembling knees but kept his spine straight and made a slight bow. "How may I be of service, your excellence?"

Zhang Wei studied the man before him and wondered if he'd been too hasty in removing the lieutenant's hand. This man was not cowed by his disability but showed grace and pride, in spite of it.

Clearing his throat, Zhang Wei said, "I see you have survived your punishment, Chin. I am happy for you."

Again, Lee gave a slight bow, and answered, "Thank you, sir. I live only to serve."

"Good!" Zhang declared. "I have a job for you." He stood

up and started pacing the room. Glaring in Lee's direction, he added, "I want vengeance for the loss of my son, but this funeral is taking up all my time. You would think that a man in my position would be able to set his own schedule, but tradition flows strong in our blood."

The supreme ruler turned around abruptly and sat back down behind his desk. "So, I want you to go to the city of Wenatchee. I want you to appear as a beggar." Zhang grinned. "Frankly, I assumed that wouldn't be hard for you, considering…" he gestured toward Lee's missing hand.

Seeing the cold, still look on Lee's face, Zhang sobered, and said, "You will be a beggar for me and thus, invisible to the people who live there. While you do that, you will be my eyes and my ears. You will be on the look-out for a woman named Sweetie Mack, and any companions she might have.

"Then, once you find her, you will wire me with your intelligence. As I said, I can't make a move until my son is buried, which will be in a little over a week's time. Meanwhile, I need to track my enemies down. I have men in the city of Spokane who will be looking for the man known as Matthew Wilcox, even as you locate the woman who conspired to bring me low."

The old man sighed and for the first time, Lee saw sorrow darken Zhang's features. Then, as if sensing Lee's regard, he sat up straight and added, "Once the funeral is over, I will send my best assassins to erase the woman, Wilcox, and all their friends from the face of the earth."

Zhang's eyes settled on his former lieutenant, and he murmured, "If you pull this off, Chin, I will consider you forgiven and reinstate you as one of my top lieutenants."

Again, Lee gave a respectful nod and tried to look enthusiastic, but his heart had shriveled in shame, along with his arm, and his pride. He managed, barely, to look grateful and then he replied, "It is my humble honor, exalted leader, to do your bidding."

38

Billy Drake stood staring out his office window at the teeming riot of cattle moving along the street in front of his home. He glared and mumbled, "I'm gonna shut that man down!"

Apparently, one of the biggest cattle ranchers in Chelan County, Clive Hancock, had decided to move his herd east to west through the city proper rather than follow the northern route – away from the city streets – that Billy had ordered built for that very purpose.

Clive had a fairly large herd; over six hundred head, and the mess they made moving through the city was unbelievable. They stank up the neighborhood, pummeled fences, and ran rampant over well-kempt lawns and alleys alike.

However, going straight west from Clive's ranch was about thirty miles shorter...and Clive was willing to risk the mayor's wrath in expediently delivering his cattle to summer pasture. *Well, we'll see about that!* Billy fumed and sat at his desk to make a telephone call.

He called his police chief and told the man to round-up Clive and all his hands and throw them in jail; his cattle could rot for all Billy cared. After he hung up, he stared at the far wall.

Where in the hell are Kenny and David? he fretted. He'd sent them out to assassinate Roger and Denny five days ago, and he hadn't heard a peep out of them since. Had they accomplished their mission! Or, had Roger and Denny done them in? He shook his head. Not knowing was driving him loco.

In addition, no matter how many times he sent agitators to The Lucky Lady Saloon, they were either stopped outright by the vast security team the owners had assembled or came away so bloody they were unwilling to participate further in Billy's schemes to shut the place down.

Even his bought and paid-for sheriffs and deputies had started to grumble. Many citizens were questioning their police force and expressing doubts about their competence. It didn't help matters that every lawman in the county knew that elections were coming up soon.

They simply couldn't understand Billy's animosity toward the new business, and no longer wanted to stand behind the bums and ne'er do wells he sent to the saloon every day.

Billy wanted to kill every one of those smug law-dogs, but respectability came at a price. He could no longer just rid himself of every person who bothered him...that would entail murdering half the town, and he was smart enough to know that bad mayors were strung-up and hanged on a regular basis. He didn't want to be the next crooked mayor to kick air at the hands of his irate citizens.

He sighed, wondering if over confidence was bringing his plans down. First, he'd trusted Sammy Chen, as an old friend, to do his part in relieving The Lucky Lady's owners of their cash, but that had fallen through. Apparently, childhood friendships carried no water when it came to the Tong. Depending on the good will of another man was a mistake he would never make again.

In fact...he grabbed a pen and jotted down a note about having Sammy meet an unfortunate accident. Although the two scamps he'd sent to get rid of Denny and Roger hadn't checked in yet, they probably would pretty soon. He'd send those two, since they seemed to have no qualms about ending a life.

He also made a note to have a couple of his deputies pay Clive Hancock a late-night visit. Maybe a couple of broken legs would convince the old coot that going against Willian Darcy's wishes was hazardous to one's peace of mind, not to mention his health!

✳✳✳

Later on that same day, Chin Lee and his mother stepped down off the train in Wenatchee. Lee was surprised that Zhang Wei had allowed his mother to accompany him, but the supreme ruler must have realized that at this time, Lee's bodily functions were limited, and he needed help for even the simplest tasks, like dressing, cooking and eating.

He was ill as they left the train station; so nauseated and pain-filled, he hardly noticed the beautiful surroundings. He simply sat back in the hired carriage, closed his eyes and allowed his mother to conduct his business transactions. They made their way downtown to a room they'd let and, once there, Lee lay down on one of the two beds and fell deeply asleep.

He woke up about fours later to the smell of tea and noodles. His mother had been busy and wasted no time in starting a fire in the little cookstove. In fact, the room was so warm from her efforts, his body was covered in sweat, and he awoke with a growl of discomfort.

When he complained, however, she arched an eyebrow and said, "Those poisons in your body must be sweated out, my son. You must work hard now to get your strength back; and your honor. This is your chance, and I will help you do that."

Frowning, Lee sighed and stared at the ceiling over his bed. The nap he'd just taken was working wonders; both physically, and mentally. He'd been so filled with shame and sorrow after his hand was removed and he lost his position with the Tong, all he really desired was to die. Now, though, away from the close confines of his own home and angry wives, he was starting to look forward to life again.

Part of it was due to his indefatigable mama-san, but most of his new-found confidence came from the realization that he no longer feared Zhang Wei. The supreme leader had taken his strong right hand; thinking, no doubt, that it was his leading hand, but it wasn't. Lee was and had always been ambidextrous.

In addition, his boss's cruelty had dealt a fatal blow to any loyalty Lee had once felt for the Tong. Sure, he acknowledged, the man was angry and grieving over the loss of his son, but Lee had seen Zhang Wei use extreme violence one too many times; rage-filled actions that hurt his friends as well as his enemies.

Well, he thought, *I'm away from him now, and I intend to stay away!*

He knew that Zhang Wei had most likely sent his *boo how doy* to the Wenatchee area to keep tabs on him. But Lee had not risen to the rank of Lieutenant for being stupid. He knew a hundred ways to hide from their prying eyes. He knew how to speak and write English, which most of the soldiers did not, and he also had much of the fortune he'd amassed over the years, hidden away here in one of his mother's teapots.

Many of the Tong soldiers could be bought, he knew, and he intended to do just that to bring Zhang Wei down! First thing first…he needed to find the Mack woman and tell her about the assassins coming her way, and then, he needed to find that Wilcox man and give him the same intelligence.

Who knows? he thought with a slight grin. *Maybe they will be so grateful, they will help to pad my fortune, so my mother and I can fly away, back to California, and into the open arms of Zhang Weis' most vicious rivals- the Yakuza!*

PART FIVE

A JUSTIFIABLE ENDING

39

Sweetie smiled as she looked again at the books. For the first time in over a month, her restaurant/saloon was showing a profit. The turn-around had begun a few days after she and Steven returned from Granville. Mainly, because the daily assaults on the premises had ceased.

She didn't know why. Had Billy gotten bored with his own harassment? Had the roughnecks who carried out his orders given up when faced with their own hired security? She didn't know, and really didn't care. All she knew was maybe, just maybe, she could actually settle down here with her new business.

This place had the potential to last many years, and to serve this community with honor and integrity...to become a landmark. Gazing out the window at the good, rich soil and boundless fruit trees that smelled like heaven, she hoped with all her heart that she could stay here forever.

She heard a knock at the door, and called out, "Come in!"

A moment later, Trask and Matthew stepped inside

her office. Both were wearing small smiles, and Sweetie couldn't help but grin in return. Trask and Matthew had bonded immediately, becoming fast friends the minute Matthew and his son stepped off the train a couple of weeks ago and were met by Trask and Randall Winters.

After leaving the train station the four men had gone to a small café in Wenatchee and had pie and coffee. This had given Trask the opportunity to size Sweetie's friends up and see if they were on the level. Apparently, they met his exacting standards and by the time their carriage pulled in front of The Lucky Lady, the four men were fast friends.

This relieved Sweetie no end – the last thing she needed at this point was suspicion and mistrust between her top lieutenants and the private eye she had hired to look into Billy Drake and what remained of his old crew.

The smiles on their faces was a relief as well. This told her that Matthew had enjoyed a successful day in rounding up witnesses to William Darcy's many crimes. Trask had been grinning a lot lately...bringing in more security had been his idea and seeing how the restaurant was faring – both intact and in the black – made him feel as though he was successful in protecting his boss and her concerns.

After the men sat down, she stood and said, "Can I buy you two a drink?"

Both men nodded and she poured a couple of fingers of whiskey in three glasses. Serving the men their drinks, she said, "Okay, tell me!"

She sat back down at her desk and listened as Trask

spoke. "Still no sign of trouble, Sweetie. I have men posted all up and down this street, and no one has seen anything out of the ordinary. Plus, we're hearing that there will be a big crowd here on Saturday because of that musician you hired. The bar is stocked up good, and Curtis has decided to serve fried chicken and tater salad-picnic-style. Since the weather's so warm, he figured there would be a lot of spill over into the backyard, so the boys are setting up tables outside."

To her bemusement, Trask was turning into a better than average restaurateur. She was surprised because Trask had always been in the military, and she thought the finer points of running a successful restaurant would be beneath his dignity. However, he seemed to have a feel for what would make the customers happy; it also didn't hurt that he ran the place with military precision.

She smiled, dipped her head, and said, "That's great Edwin. As always, you're doing an excellent job."

He sat back in his chair with a pleased expression and sipped his whiskey as Sweetie turned to Matthew. "And, what about you, Matthew. Any more good news?"

He nodded. "Yes, I have two more people lined up and more than ready to stand as witnesses. That makes six men and women of good standing who will testify against Billy Drake and his henchmen." He grinned, adding, "That makes six...four more, and I will call both the U S Marshals and the Pinkertons."

Sweetie grinned at his excitement but sobered almost

immediately. "Anyone hear about the Tong? I've been sleeping with my heart in my throat for a couple of weeks now, thinking that Chinese assassins are lurking in every shadow."

"That makes three of us, Sweetie," Matthew answered. But no, nothing yet. I have Chance, Tommy and a few others keeping tabs on the train station and the three stagecoach stations in the area...but it's hard to tell what's going on there. I didn't realize how big and busy this train station is. That's an issue because a lot of Chinese work the rails. Just in this town alone, there are six old train cars set aside for the railroad workers. They are parked in a siding, away from the working trains, but a whole shantytown has sprung up around those cars."

Sweetie looked shocked. "You know, it's almost funny how I take rail travel for granted. I never realized that so many Chinese workers actually become a part of the rail-road system."

Matthew sighed. "Well, it's actually worse than that. Remember that many Chinese workers are no less than in-dentured servants. A lot of them come here because they've heard rumors about how this land is paved with gold. So, they go all-in, straight from China but the odds are stacked against them from the start. Often, they are flat-broke once they hit our shoreline and that's when unscrupulous bro-kers step in, make false promises, and basically hire their own personal slaves for a profit. It's a fact, Sweetie, sad but true."

Trask nodded in agreement. "It happens everywhere, Sweetie. From Negro slaves, to Mexicans migrants, white sailors who are 'Shanghaied' into service and the Chinese. The strong subjugate the weak. A sorry fact of life."

Sweetie shook her head. "So, how will we even know if the Tong soldiers are coming for us? How many Chinese people live in and around that little shantytown, Matthew? Do you know?"

He shook his head. "Hundreds...maybe closer to a thousand. It's hard to tell. Chance did say, though, that there's some whispering about a Tong bigwig showing up recently. Those people know authority when they see it, but apparently, this new guy is keeping his head down. He may be a precursor to a Tong attack, but right now, the jury's out. He may just be a man who is here to take some control over this little Chinatown...who knows?"

The three friends sat and thought about things for a moment, and then Trask said, "Do you think it might be a good thing to go and seek an audience with this man? Maybe he'll try to attack us where we stand, but we have an army of our own – a small one, perhaps, but capable all the same. Maybe we can beard the goat by approaching him first?"

Sweetie looked aghast, but then her gaze sharpened, and she said, "What do you think, Matthew? Is it worth a shot?"

Matthew just smiled.

40

Billy Drake paced back and forth in his office like a caged lion. Punching his right fist into his left, he growled out loud. "Where in the hell are they?" He was thinking about the two young men he'd sent out to kill Denny and Roger. "Dead, probably, dammit!" he continued. "But, if so, what happened to Denny and Roger? Did they put my two gunners down, and flee? Or…" He spun on his heel and headed back toward the window to peer outside. "…are those two gunnin' for me now? Dammit!"

Wishing his two best men were nearby, he shook his head. Apparently, after Clive and his cowhands were released from jail, Kevin Woolsey and Pete Meadows had knee-capped the elderly rancher. Billy clenched his fists in frustration. It was too much – the doc had informed one of Billy's spies that Hancock would never walk again – but that's what you got when you put Pete in charge of things; violence in the extreme. Kevin wasn't as bad, but he was a follower – always had been – and when Pete said, "Kill!" by

God, that's what Kevin would do.

Unfortunately, however, Hancock's hired hands had gone, en mass, to the Lucky Lady Saloon and volunteered information to a man named Matthew Wilcox. They were incensed by the mayor's brutal actions and vowed to bring the man they knew as William Darcy down; if it was the last thing they ever did.

Matthew was jubilant. He now had fourteen people willing and eager to stand witness to Drake's crimes, and that was more than enough to tempt both the U.S. Marshals and the Pinkertons to get involved in the take down. *That is, if the people of this fair town don't string Billy up first!*

Matthew had been a lawman for a long time, most of his life really and had seen "Mob Action" more than a few times. Just thinking about it made his blood run cold. No matter how aggrieved a person, or a group of people felt by injustices raining down on them and the folks they loved, too many innocents got hurt in riots or 'mob rule'.

Besides, he admitted, *Drake is Sweetie's prize.* He figured she would eventually get over losing her prize to a lynching; but hopefully, if the Marshals or the Pinks were here to quell any rebellions, she would see the man hang for the crimes Drake had committed against her and her family so long ago.

Glaring down at the empty street now, however, Drake had no way of knowing about the witnesses lining up against him or that the legal noose was tightening around his throat. He was more worried about retribution coming his way from the men he'd tried to assassinate. Denny was a buffoon and couldn't hit a barn wall unless he had a scatter gun in his hands. If Denny *had* survived, Drake's security team would be on him the minute he rode back into town.

Roger, though...Billy shuddered suddenly, as if a goose had just walked over his grave. That man was dangerous. A better than average shot, a mean brawler, and sporting a thirst for violence, Billy had not seen since his friend Eddie Machete had gone under.

As Billy made plans to shore-up his own personal security, a furtive motion caught his eye. Hair raising on the back of his neck, he stepped sideways and peeked out from behind the silk drapes framing the window. Two... no, three men stepped out from the hedgerow surrounding his neighbors' house.

From his angle, they looked like small men, no more than 5'8 at most, and his reckoning was correct, for as he stared, he noticed their black pants, mid-length black tunics and long hair which was bound tightly to their heads.

Not for nothing, Billy had spent a lot of time with Sammy and his family when he was a child. He'd been fascinated by the *boo how doy* that showed up in Chinatown on occasion and had begged Sammy to explain their function and lethality. Eager to share his own social history, Sammy had complied and spoke of what he knew of the ancient Samurai soldiers, the modern-day *boo how doy,* the Tong and Yakuza assassins and the many "fighting" lieutenants that comprised the gang's hierarchy.

He remembered being excited and more than impressed when his young friend filled him in on the Chinese soldiers but now, seeing the three Chinamen "dressed to kill" just across the street from where he resided, his heart clinched in fear and dread.

He wondered frantically, had his boys laid Sammy low? Did they actually kill his old friend or had Sammy survived long enough to sic his war dogs on him? Drake took a breath and peered down at the three Oriental men who were now standing side by side and gazing at the front of his red-brick mansion.

My God! he thought and stepped behind the heavy drapes. Then, he leaned sideways and picked up a small brass bell that sat on the edge of his desk. Almost immediately his head of security, Mike Adams, opened the door to Drake's office and said, "You rang, boss?"

"Yes! I think we're under attack. I need you to bring every man up here to guard me. While you do that, I'm going to bring more men in from downtown. Now, Hurry!"

Looking stricken, Mike called out, "Hey, you three, come up here right away!" Within seconds, Drake heard a clamor of footfalls on the staircase and then the four men stood in Billy's office, looking white-eyed and nervous.

Feeling marginally safer, Drake called his headquarters; the old Beer Stine Tavern – a play on words invented by Sweetie's new barkeeps, Marty and Ron Stine when they still owned and operated the place. He told the bartender on duty to send five of his best men to his house, *pronto!* Then, he turned to Mike and said, "I need you to go to the window and see if they're still there."

Mike hesitated, looking a little green around the gills. "Who's they, boss? What am I looking for?"

Drake barked, "You'll know it when you see it! Now, go look outside but be careful. Hide behind the curtain so they don't see you."

Looking as if he'd rather be doing anything, anything at all besides going to the window, Mike tiptoed to the edge of the drapes and peeked outside. He looked and looked some more as Billy and the rest of his men shifted in nervous anticipation. Then he said, "Uh boss? There's no one out there. The street is empty."

Billy gaped and stepped toward the other side of the window. Looking down he saw that, indeed, the street in front of his home was completely deserted. Fury took over the fear he'd felt only moments earlier and he snapped, "Well, they were there, I tell you."

Mike nodded but couldn't help but ask, "Sorry, sir, but just to be clear, who were they? What do me and the boys need to look out for?"

Billy sat down in his chair with a sigh. "Assassins, that's who. Chinese assassins. Pack your gear up boys, we're heading down to the bar. Safety in numbers, you know."

As the men paused to see if he needed anything else, Drake turned on them with a roar of rage, and screamed, "NOW!"

41

Chance Wilcox and his new friend Tom Kirwin were ready to give up on their search for the mysterious power-player in the little Chinatown by the railroad siding. Both of them were big men, especially Tommy who stood close to 6'5 and weighed over 250 pounds.

Chance was also tall; standing at 6'1 and weighing in at about 205 pounds of lean muscle. They were both handsome, clean-cut and well-dressed. It didn't matter, though. As soon as the two men got anywhere near the people living close to the old train cars, the Celestials would gasp and scatter like a covey of quail. They found themselves shouting out questions about the new Tong leader in their midst, which only served to startle the Chinese even more.

So, after three days of trying to track the man down, they finally gave up and went back to the Lucky Lady Saloon to report to Matthew and Trask. They sipped coffee as they discussed their failure, but Matthew was not angry or worried. He'd been busy with his own investigation and now thought that, maybe, the Tong threat had been overstated.

They might come, he thought, but if things go as planned, there will soon be so many lawmen in town, even the Tong will hesitate to act. After all, the Tong were criminals and constantly under investigation by a number of federal agencies; including the ones that would be showing up within the next few days.

Shrugging off his doubts, he said, "That's okay, boys, it was a long shot anyway. Say, would the two of you help with security today? Apparently, there's huge crowd coming to see the band, and I worry that Darcy's rabble-rousers may make another appearance."

Both men agreed, and Tommy asked, "Did I hear that an Irish band is coming to perform?"

Trask nodded with a smile. "Yes. They call themselves the Irish Songsters, and I hear they're really good."

Tommy grinned. "Were you aware that there's a pretty big Irish community here in the Valley? Ten or twelve families, at least, along with all their friends and extended relatives. Hell, half of my kin are Irish."

Trask smiled in return. "Well, I heard something along those lines...why do you think I asked the band to come?"

The men chuckled, marveling at what a good businessman the retired soldier was turning out to be. Then, they heard a shout from outside and Trask stepped to the window. Peering down, he said, "Speaking of Irishmen, here's the band. Let's go and see if they need a hand setting up, eh?"

✳

Had either Chance or his father known that their quarry was residing less than a hundred feet away and milking one of the saloon's four goats, they would have fallen over in shock. But Chin (Lucky) Lee had come to the saloon looking for work ten days earlier, and had been hired by the restaurant's chef, Bradley Gooding, to help care for the small herd of milk cows, sheep and goats the kitchen used to supplement their menus.

The cows were placid, but the goats were a handful and had bitten or kicked Nina's grandchildren more than once when they tried to harvest the beasts' milk for cheese. Lucky had told the chef that he was an old hand at handling goats, which was nothing less than the truth. As a child, Chin Lee had taken care of most of his village's animals before his mother and father had relocated the family to America.

Gooding had looked, askance, at Lee's missing right hand but Lee had demonstrated the strength and dexterity of his talented left hand, and he was hired on the spot. Since then, he had moved into the animals' small shelter and went about his job with grace and efficiency. He wore old black pants and a tattered, threadbare tunic that was gray with age.

Thus, he thought with a sly grin, *I look like an old bum, per Zhang Wei's wishes, but I'm also in a unique position to find Sweetie Mack and her business partner, Matthew Wilcox.*

Zhang Weis' soldiers were aware of his relocation and had informed their boss but had been told to let Lee be. Zhang figured his old lieutenant was getting close to his American enemies in order to be on hand when the *boo how doy* stepped in to murder them. Unfortunately, for Zhang Wei, Lee had no intention of letting the Tong leader know about their whereabouts, just so he could send his assassins to kill them off. Rather, he was there to warn the man and woman of an impending attack. He had found Mr. Wilcox right away but not yet found the right time to approach the man with his intelligence.

After all, an old Chink would not be welcome to roam the premises when he should be minding the livestock, and neither Matthew nor his son Chance visited the barnyard. Lee had recently, however, been allowed into the horse barn, where he helped water, feed and groom the owner's mounts. Wilcox and his son *did* go to the horse barn regularly, and Lee meant to speak to one of them as soon as possible.

As for the woman, Sweetie Mack, Chin Lee had no clue. The only women around this saloon was an old Italian grandma, a few waitresses, a couple of kitchen wenches, and a few female children. There was no evil mastermind in women's clothing hanging about that he could see.

There *was* a rather effeminate young man who descended the stairs on occasion to visit with the kitchen staff. He was tall and gawky, with wispy brown hair and large round spectacles that made him look like a scrawny owl. Lee snorted and rolled his eyes.

Lucky rather liked the American people, unlike most of the Tong leaders and the *boo how doy*, but they *did* act in a most peculiar way sometimes. Thinking that the boy was a poof boy, and shuddering with disgust, he suddenly remembered his own cousin who loved to wear his mother's kimonos and make-up.

That boy had stated often and loudly that he would make a better woman than any man and had persisted in his outspoken remarks until the day his father packed him up and deposited him in a monastery, over a hundred miles away from their village.

Lee had liked the child and had missed him sorely after he disappeared. So, he decided now not to hate the spindly young man named Martin, who seemed to haunt the back stairs and only came out in public surrounded by his brother, the boss who was called Trask, and an old black man named Randall Winters.

Lee finished milking the goat and wiped his hand on a towel. *Now, Winters is a good, good man,* he thought. He'd been working here for almost two weeks and not a day went by that the old Negro didn't step outside to offer Lee and the other employees a treat from the kitchen or a beverage from the bar. Twice, Winters had brought a steaming bowl of rice out from the kitchen for Lee's lunch, and Lee seriously doubted that rice was on the restaurant's regular menu.

If fact, all the people working here seemed to be nice

people, kind and warm. It was Zhang Wei who was evil and cruel. Lee thought again about the Tong leader and how much he would enjoy seeing him put down, when a sound filled the air. A sound that took him back to his youth.

Two flutes and a violin wailed in unison, and the music they made brought tears to the old lieutenant's eyes. It was the sound of sorrow and joy, heartache and triumph, life and death.

The Irish had come to the Lucky Lady Saloon.

42

Oh, Danny Boy
The pipes, the pipes are calling
From glen to glen
And down the mountainside

The summer's gone
And all the roses falling
It's you, it's you must go
And I must bide.

But come ye back when
Summer's in the meadow
Or when the valley's hushed
And white with snow

It's I'll be here in
Sunshine or in shadow
Oh, Danny boy, oh, Danny boy

I love you so,

Oh, Danny boy, oh, Danny boy
I love you so.

The entertainment at The Lucky Lady saloon had started hours earlier. Carriage after carriage, buggies, and wagons had been rolling in all afternoon long, and by 5:00 there was standing room only within the restaurant. Many folks had spilled out onto the backyard then, and were met with tables of fried chicken, potato salad, red beans, garden-fresh buttery Brussel sprouts, sliced tomatoes, and apple pie.

Eventually, the band moved outside as well. They sang of the old country with a poignancy that was almost overwhelming; songs like, The Ballad of the Irish Horse, Whiskey in a Jar, The Gypsy Rover, The Galway Girl, Molly Malone and The Fields of Athenry...which left no dry eye in the crowd.

Trask stood by a stand of aspen trees, smoking his pipe and looking like the cat that ate the cream. He glanced up at the window and winked at Sweetie, who stood looking down at the dwindling crowd with a small smile. She was thinking, *hiring the band was a stroke of genius on Edwin's part.*

Many of the people who had come today had tears of joy in their eyes when they finally took their leave. They, or their folks had left the old country to seek a better life, but most missed their homeland, and mourned its continued misfortune. People there were still starving, and under harsh rule, which made their American cousins weep with pity.

Although, as usual, Sweetie remained hidden from prying eyes, she had heard that more than a few customers swore that they would bring their custom to The Lucky Lady, exclusively, from now on despite the mayor's wishes.

Lately, William Darcy's popularity had taken a hard hit. It was any number of things; but when some of the most influential citizens heard that Darcy's henchmen had crippled their good friend, Clive Hancock, they had agreed privately but unanimously that the mayor was a rotten egg and had to go. Elections were coming up soon, and they vowed to rid the mayoral seat of the odious corruption and unbridled power William Darcy represented and wasn't afraid to use.

The band was packing up now and heading inside for a well-earned dinner and a few drinks, leaving only a few people outside. Some of them – younger couples mainly – continued to dance and sway to a tune only they could hear, and a few groups of men huddled together exchanging news and small talk. It was a little after eight in the evening and daylight was fading, shadows growing long as the sun dipped below the tree line.

Staring, Sweetie saw Matthew and Chance talking to someone by the far side of the bonfire the kitchen staff had started up earlier for the guests' amusement. *Who is that?* she wondered, and then stepped back as both Matthew and his son turned abruptly and stared up at where she stood.

Looking through the dusky shadows, Sweetie saw that the man they were talking to was their new hired man. *What's his name, again?* she mused. *Lee... yes, Chin Lee.* The man usually looked bent and as stooped over as an old mule but now, for some reason, he seemed to stand much taller.

He gazed up at her and bowed slightly, as if to say, *I know you, and acknowledge your part in this...*

Heart speeding up suddenly, Sweetie opened her window and called down in her deepest voice, "Matthew? What is it?"

He took a few steps and looking up, answered, "We need to talk. Immediately, if possible."

Looking doubtful, she said, "Okay, come on up." Then she closed the door and went to the highboy to check on her mustache and don her spectacles. Before she'd closed the window, Sweetie saw all three men heading toward the building, so she figured Lee was coming upstairs to meet with her as well.

Well, I hope Matthew knows what he's doing! She knew her cover would be blown eventually but didn't figure it would be right now, tonight!

A few minutes passed and then came a knock on the door. "Come!" she said, and the three men stepped inside along with her friend Steven Mercer. Her friends seemed nervous, but the Oriental man seemed serene, almost joyful.

"Sit please, gentlemen...and, Matthew, this had better be good," she added with an edge to her voice.

Glancing her way, Matthew nodded and replied, "Oh, it's not good, but it's news you need to hear."

"Great," she sighed. Now that the men were seated, she stared directly at the rather handsome, one-handed middle-aged Chinese man who had seemed so old and frail when he first hired on, but now seemed as stout and strong as an oak tree. "Well, who are you, really, Mister Lee? Or is that even your name?"

Lee dipped his head, and said, "Chin Lee *is* my name, Miss...I mean Martin. But I have come to your establishment under false pretenses."

She glared at him and he cleared his throat, "Please, I have come to warn you, and to help if I can!"

Sweetie continued to frown, but something in the man's eyes convinced her that he was on the level. Although she had no clue why an old goatherd would trouble himself in her affairs, she decided to give him a shot at explaining. "Okay, talk."

Lee took a deep breath and then said, "As I said before, my name is Chin Lee and I was once a lieutenant for the Tong in both Seattle and San Francisco. I was in good standing with our leader, Zhang Wei until some of his *boo how doy* stole a strongbox that, I believe, belonged to you... Miss Sweetie Mack."

Sweetie felt shock run through her veins. She had barely even noticed the man her chef had hired a couple weeks earlier. How had he figured out that she was a woman in disguise? And, the *Tong!* Had this man actually infiltrated her establishment with designs to kill her and her friends? Who had sent him, and more importantly, what did he want!

Matthew saw Sweetie's shock and her struggle to understand what she was facing. He said, "Sweetie, this man is here to warn us of an imminent attack. He was tortured by the Tong leader, and is taking a huge risk in coming to us, okay?"

Sweetie swallowed the lump of nerves in her throat and nodded. Taking off her glasses and peeling the itchy mustache off her upper lip she said, "Please forgive me, Mister Lee. You took me by surprise. Go on with your story and I'll listen."

Lee sat still for moment as if collecting his thoughts and then said, "I spoke to Mister Wilcox earlier, and he told me that neither of you knew or authorized the use of rattlesnakes in the strongbox you sent to Seattle. Is that correct?"

Sweetie shook her head. "Of course not. That would have put everyone I know in terrible danger. Mister Wilcox's own son was supposed to bring that box to the Spokane area...why would I endanger him?"

Lee nodded. "You see, that changes everything. My boss, Zhang Wei, thought it was some sort of trick; something personal designed to ruin his life. He took his son's death hard and naturally, made immediate plans to terminate the box's owners."

Sweetie just shook her head. Turning to Matthew, she murmured, "I'd like to shoot that forger I hired. What a fool

I was..."

Smiling, Lee said, "If you would permit me to make a phone call? I think I can call the Tong leader's dogs, if I move quickly."

Sweetie nodded, and said, "Please do, and thank you!"

He picked up the phone, waited a moment and then spoke softly into the handset. Sweetie heard the Chinese tongue and wished she could understand what the man was saying, when a piercing scream cut through the night air.

43

A few hours earlier, Billy Drake was sitting in the old Beer Stine bar getting stinking drunk. He stared into his glass and thought about how everything was going wrong – starting with the grand opening of The Lucky Lady Saloon.

He hated those people with a passion so strong it had caused him to make poor choices. He knew this, but refused to acknowledge his own culpability, preferring rather, to blame the Lucky Lady for his woes.

Now, because of those California upstarts, he had the Tong after him (maybe; at least he thought so); he had needed to rid himself of a couple of his own men and had probably lost two more in the assassination attempt. His two best men, Pete and Kevin, were out of town, ostensibly doing some chores for him in the Seattle area but actually hiding out from the irate citizens of Wenatchee. And now, adding insult to injury, word had come down that major players in Chelan County were plotting to take his mayoral seat away.

It's the Luck Lady's fault! he fumed. *One light in the darkness is the fact that Kevin and Pete are due to arrive back home within the hour.* Depending on whether the train was on time or not, having a part of his old gang by his side made Billy breathe a little easier. *Speaking of darkness...* taking a slug off his glass, he glared about at the bar and got pissed all over again. "Bring me another shot!" he barked, adding, "Where the hell is everybody tonight?"

He hiccupped and stared about at the empty bar as a couple of his men exchanged guarded glances. "Well?" Billy added, "It's six-thirty on a Saturday night. This place should be hopping but it's as deserted as a graveyard! Looks like you men don't know how to run a bar!"

One of the bartenders, a kid named Spence, squeaked, "It's the Luck Lady, boss. We heard that they brought in some sort of famous Irish band to entertain...we also heard that the place is crammed full! Sorry, but it ain't our fault! We've been running a happy hour with pickled eggs and pig's feet every night and even giving out free booze to those what show up! We're really trying..."

"Free booze! You gotta be kidding me!" Billy roared and his face flushed beet-red. He was not in the bar business to give away free *anything*, but damn! *It's those people at the Lucky Lady, again!* he thought as the room started swirling around him. He was inebriated but, as usual, too arrogant to admit that he was in no shape to make another rash decision regarding his competition.

Standing up and trying to act as upright and sober as a

priest in a pulpit, he hissed, "That's it. I've had it. As soon as Pete and Kevin show up, we'll round the rest of the boys up, and then go and shut that place down for good!"

Always ready and eager to participate in a dust-up with the locals who had, after all, rejected them and their co-horts, the "boys" stared at their boss and then at one anoth-er. "Uh...Mister Darcy," Mike Adams stuttered, "Your men are all here, best I can recall."

Billy stared about at his security force and realized, sud-denly, that he'd been slack and let his personal security team dwindle down to almost nothing. Most of the dirty cops on his payroll were on duty tonight and couldn't be expected to participate in a riot against their own citizens.

But, unfortunately, the men in the bar with him now were not the best or toughest of his regular team. "Dam-mit!" he growled under his breath, and squinting into the bar's dim light, he saw that only six men were guarding him. *Not enough!* he realized with a sick feeling in his gut.

Still, though, resentment and fury filled his heart. Nine men, counting Pete, Kevin and himself, could do a lot of damage to the saloon and the people who ran it, especially if their guard was down and they were made vulnerable by the presence of paying customers!

Feeling a boozy thrill, he hollered, "We got plenty of men...enough to do some real damage if we get a move on. Pete and Kevin will be here real soon. Then, we're gonna go kick some ass!"

The men in the bar managed to muster a weak "hurrah!", although it was a matter of good form rather than any exuberance over their boss' latest scheme.

Drake continued to gulp whiskey until Pete and Kevin sauntered in about twenty minutes later. It took fifteen minutes to load up two wagons with guns, knives, saps and extra ammunition. Then, another ten minutes passed as the men wrestled their skunk-drunk boss into the carriage. Finally, they were off to wreak as much damage as possible on the Lucky Lady saloon and its owners.

As this took place, a dark, skinny shadow watched with narrow, calculating gray eyes.

✳✳✳

Hearing that dreadful scream, Matthew, Trask and Chance rushed to the window and stared down into the yard. It was full-dark now, only the dwindling light of the bonfire illuminating dusk's shadows. Still, Matthew could see a number of men fighting by the tree line and one woman being dragged off into the shrubbery. They could also hear shouts and cries of pain coming up the stairs from within the restaurant itself.

Turning to Sweetie, he barked, "You stay here, and lock the door. There's some sort of brawl going on, and I want you to stay safe."

Frowning, Sweetie said, "Hey, I can take care of myself!" but Matthew shook his finger and hissed, "Do as I say, Sweetie, right now!"

She flushed, thinking, *No one has talked to me that way since my dad was still alive,* but realized, even as she struggled with her own temper, that Matthew meant business. She actually thought that if she didn't comply with his wishes immediately, he would truss her up like a goose and throw her in a closet!

Steven took her arm and whispered, "Listen to the man, Sweetie. Let them help you..."

Glaring, Sweetie shook him off, but acquiesced with a grunt of resentment. "Okay, sheesh!" She walked around her desk and took her seat, even as Chin Lee vowed to keep her and Steven safe. "Please, though, if it is the Tong, send someone up here to let me know. I know how they fight and can help you!"

Nodding, Matthew, Trask, Chance and Steven stepped out onto the landing to quell whatever new threat was menacing Sweetie's saloon and the fair citizens of Chelan County.

44

The four men crept to the bannister and peering down, saw that a full-scale brawl was taking place downstairs. Chairs and tables were flying through the air and a number of men were exchanging fists; biting, grabbing and generally kicking each other's butts.

Sighing, Trask said, "I *knew* it was too good to be true."

Matthew asked, "What's too good to be true?"

Trask said, "We haven't heard hide nor hair out of Darcy's crew lately, but I recognize a lot of them down there. Came to bust up the party, I reckon."

"Well, we'd better go and shut 'em down."

Trask frowned, nodding. "Yup, let's do it." Turning to Steven, he added, "I want you to go to your room, okay?"

Steven looked offended. "Hey! I have the right to fight, too! I might not be as good a fighter as you, Edwin, but don't deny me the right to defend Sweetie!"

Trask bit his lip and noticing that Matthew and his son Chance were already making their way downstairs, he sighed, "Steven, do as you like, but Sweetie won't thank me if you get hurt. Maybe...why don't you try and get the innocents out of here? Dash behind the bar and lead the waitstaff through the kitchen and out the back door. That would be really helpful."

Looking relieved, Steven nodded. "Just let me go to my room and grab my pistol. I'll be right back." He turned on his heel and ran to his office. Unwilling to wait, Trask moved swiftly down the stairs and saw most of the action had moved outside. Looked to him like Drake's boys just wanted to shake things up a bit, rather than cause real damage, which was a good thing.

At least there was no gunplay, yet. Just as that thought occurred to him, however, Trask heard a pistol shot. "Dammit to hell!" he swore and, pulling his own gun, made his way through the kitchen. He saw a number of employees hiding behind shelves and tucked behind assorted barrels and sacks in the storeroom.

Trask locked the kitchen door and whispered loudly, "You guys stay hidden here until Steven or I come back in to get you!" Then, he opened the back door and peered outside. A lot of the fights had broken up after the gunshot and both men and women stood about in nervous clusters, wide-eyed and trembling.

Looking past them into the shrubbery, he thought he saw Matthew's tall form framed in moonlight, his still smoking pistol sagging in his right hand. Trask ran across the lawn and met up with the man who was toeing his boot into the ribs of a fat, dying man. His head was shattered, and blood seeped onto the grass. Staring, Trask saw that it was one of Drake's hired guns – the man known as Kevin Woolsey.

Grunting with some disapproval, he muttered, "I know he's a bad egg, but did you have to shoot him dead? It's gonna get complicated for us now..."

Matthew glared and tipped his chin to Trask's right-hand side. Looking around, he saw a woman slumped and weeping against the chest of Matthew's son, Chance. Her bodice was ripped down the middle, exposing her breasts, which were red and weeping with claw marks. Her skirt was hiked up, and Trask understood that she'd been raped.

Turning back to face Matthew with a look of disgust on his face, he acknowledged, "Sorry, Matthew. I didn't realize."

Matthew nodded once and said, "Is the ruckus over with?"

Trask shrugged. "Seems like it. Let's go see."

Chance stayed behind to help the young woman, but Trask and Matthew stepped from the hedgerow and stared about at the yard. They both held their pistols at the ready, but the men who had swept in to break the place up seemed to have disappeared.

They saw Randall Winters going from person to person offering water and assistance, and then they saw Tommy and Bradley hauling a couple of bodies across the yard by their feet. Those men appeared to be trussed up like geese, and Trask couldn't help but grin.

A few more men were man-handling the rest of Drake's roustabouts into the barnyard, and Matthew saw that they were being tied to the rails of the corral. "Good job, fellas," he murmured in satisfaction.

He picked up a nearby lantern and made his way into the barnyard, where the chickens were running around like crazy and screaming querulous questions into the night. He turned to Trask and said, "Looky there… I think that's Billy Drake in the flesh."

Trask had only seen the man once and he had looked much different; well-oiled and pompous. But he saw now that the man who was either dead or passed out by the corral was heavy-set, red-headed, and had a mean cast to his mouth. "Yup. Looks like we netted a pretty big fish. Sweetie's gonna be happy."

Just then, Matthew saw a number of small dark shadows emerge into the back yard. Squinting into the night and trying to make sense of what his eyes were telling him, Matthew heard a loud thump and a strangled cry to his right. Cocking his gun, Matthew whirled sideways and saw that a hatchet was buried in Edwin Trask's forehead.

The old man's eyes were crossed, as though he was trying to see what had hit him and then his knees gave away and he fell to the ground, dead.

Heartsick and for the first time in years, deeply frightened, Matthew turned to face what was coming his way. He realized that the shadows were actually Tong soldiers; what

Lee had called *boo how doy. My God,* he thought as all of Sweetie's men were herded into a bunch and then he heard two things simultaneously. First, a gunshot from inside the saloon and then, his son Chance, who cried, "Pa!" as he was man-handled out from the shrubbery by even more Tong soldiers.

Even as the soldiers surrounded Matthew and forced him to his knees on the ground, a black shape separated from the others and approached. It was Chin Lee. The man he, himself, had asked to care for Sweetie Mack while he dealt with the threat. Matthew wanted to kick himself. *How stupid I was!* he marveled.

The man bowed slightly and said, "My orders are thus, Mister Wilcox. My soldiers and I will spare you, but this man…" Lee bent over and gave Drake a little poke with the sword in his hand. "This man will be delivered to Seattle to meet his fortune."

Matthew glared. "What was that gunshot I heard?"

Lee shrugged. "Miss Mack. She is dead, along with the young blond-haired man who tried to play the hero." He broke into a sunny grin, adding, "That woman actually tried to use a sword on me!" He laughed and many of his soldiers joined in his merriment.

Then he sobered and said, "I took care of them, just as I will take care of you and your son if you try and interfere with our mission."

Matthew hissed, "I trusted you! I trusted you and you betrayed us!" He tried to rise, to put his hands around the

Chinese man's neck, but the *boo how doy* beat him down to the ground.

Lee shrugged. "As always, my loyalties are to the Tong. Just be happy that I took steps to spare your life and that of your son. It could have been much, much worse." He nodded to one of the soldiers holding Chance's arm.

As Matthew watched, heart in his throat, the Chinese man drew a blade and held it to his son's neck. Panicking, he shouted, "Stop! Go ahead, take Darcy and all his men. We won't try to stop you! Just...just don't hurt my son!"

Randall Winters had crept up to where Trask lay on the ground. His eyes were leaking tears and his mouth twisted in grief. Lee's thugs sprang to attack, but Lee held up his one hand. "No! He is a good man, grieving for his friend. Leave him be!"

The soldiers stepped back obediently, and the one holding a knife to Chance's throat stepped away as well.

Turning to his men, Chin Lee barked orders in Chinese, and they dragged Billy Drake and his men away from the barnyard. Within moments, Matthew heard carriages pulling away into the night. Chance dropped to his knees and murmured, "Pa, are you hurt?"

Tears springing to his eyes, both at his son's reprieve and the sudden, terrible loss of Sweetie, Steven and her old friend Edwin Trask, he nodded silently. He heard Chance sigh with relief, and then groan as the Tong leader walked back their way.

Stooping over a little, even as police bells started ringing and rapidly approaching horse hooves tore through the air, Chin Lee spoke into Matthew's ear. "Trust not in other men's words, Mister Wilcox. Always, only, trust in your yourself. I think you have a good heart, a strong heart, and it will prevail in the end. Mister Wilcox, look at me."

Matthew refused to look up at Chin (Lucky) Lee, though, and after a moment the man turned on his heel and left.

As Lee's footsteps faded away, Matthew hung his head in defeat.

45

Chin Lee smiled as the carriage he was in made its way through the darkness to William Drake's mansion. His plan was shaping up nicely and soon he and his mamma would flee, money in hand, to a new and better life in San Francisco.

Studying Drake's face, and his miserable attempt to sober up, Lee knew that this part of the coup would be easy. After all, the man in front of him now, with his bright red face and white rolling eyes was not brave or honorable. He stood for nothing at all, except for his own petty concerns. He would give up the president of the United States if it meant he could live one more day.

Lee had no use for the man, at all, except for the fact that Billy had a fortune in gold, silver and banknotes at home in his private safe, and only *he* knew the combination of that safe. A minor annoyance, for sure, but one that could be rectified quickly.

Lee and his soldiers were heading to that safe now, and

once they pried the combination out of Drake, they would kill him and ship his head, along with those of his two top lieutenants, to Zhang Wei as proof of death. The only deviation in Zhang's plan was this trip to the man's safe.

Actually Zhang cared not about Drake's money – he only cared that the man who had, intentionally or not, set up his son's death pay the full price of his earthly mistakes. Besides, every good Tong leader expected their lieutenants to skim off the top; a small price to pay for undying loyalty.

Chin Lee was no longer loyal to Zhang Wei, but he did need Drake's money, badly, if he meant to defect to the Yakuza. He could not show up in California with his hat in his hands. He needed to make a splash. And this was the way to do it. He would pay Zhang's *boo how doy* to look the other way and be in a private carriage on his way to San Francisco with his mamma before daybreak.

The carriage rounded a corner and Drake lost his seat, tumbling to the floorboards at Lee's feet. Disdainfully, Lee kicked the man and the Tong soldier accompanying them apologized for losing his grip on the prisoner. He hauled Drake upright and Lee ordered the soldier to remove Billy's gag.

Whipping the spit-laden cloth from Billy's mouth, Lee said, "All you need to do is give me the combination to your safe. If the combination is correct and the safe opens, we will set you free."

Lee stared into Billy's frightened eyes and saw the man struggle with confusion. He was a criminal, after all, and had promised things he had no intention on delivering many times in the past. Lee could almost see the calculations going on in Drake's brain...*was the Tong leader lying or did he really have no interest in seeing him dead?*

It was almost amusing. How many times had Billy said the same thing to his many victims to get what he wanted? *Too many times to count*, Lee wagered.

Still inebriated, Billy said nothing. He only watched out the window as the carriage drew near his home. He was thinking about all the guns he had hidden away around his house. *If I can break away, for just a second, I can shoot my way out of this mess. If only my men were with me!*

But Pete was nowhere to be found and neither was Kevin. *Where in the hell did they get off to, huh?* He wondered frantically. He did not know that Kevin had met his reward at the point of Matthew Wilcox's pistol, or that Pete was being held captive by the *boo how doy* in the carriage that followed them. Billy's face flushed with rage. *Where is the loyalty, the courage to stand by their boss in his time of need? Nowhere...poof, gone, that's where!*

Lee grinned as the man's emotions played across his face like ripples on still water. Just to be mean, Lee said, "Employees often show no honor...do they, Mister Drake?"

Billy's eyes widened. *This owl-hoot knows my real name...and how in blazes did he know exactly what I was thinking just now?* Superstitious dread filled his heart and he stared at the slit-eyed man in fright.

Lee watched the man's face turn an even brighter shade

of red, and fearing he might have a heart attack before he gave up the safe's combination, he smiled gently, "Have no fear, Mister Drake. The only thing I want from you is your money. Give me the combination and I will let you live."

The carriage rolled to a stop, and Lee added, "Ah! Here we are now. Come along, Mister Drake."

Drake was pulled, none too gently, from the carriage and they made their way to the front porch. The gas porchlights were on, illuminating the shadows as Lee led the procession. Billy was followed closely by the two Tong soldiers up the cobblestone walkway. They were not holding his arms, as was the case previously, and Billy thought about the pistol hidden beneath the pot of geraniums on the front steps. *If I can just get my hands on that pistol...*

Then, something was looming in front of him – a tall, thin shadow with bared teeth, and a wicked-looking knife in his left hand. "Roger! Thank God. Help me!" was what Billy meant to say, but his words were gargled through the blood that ran in sheets down his chest.

Roger Hampsted had put as much strength as he could muster into slitting his former boss' throat, and despite the wound which was slowly killing him, his stroke almost separated Billy's head from his shoulders. In fact, Billy's head wobbled precariously as his body fell onto the pavers.

Lee turned around in surprise. Looking down at what was left of Billy's neck, his first thought was, "Well, that makes it easy to ship Drake's head to Zhang Wei, but then he heard one of his soldiers shout in rage. The stranger who had stepped out of the shadows and dispatched Drake to the seventh depths of hell, had broken away from his soldiers and was only feet away from him and moving in fast!

Lee pulled the gun he'd wrestled away from Steven Mercer out of his coat pocket and aimed it at the tall thin man with a bloody, wicked-looking knife in his hand. Before he had a chance to pull the trigger, however, he stopped abruptly and stared down at the bone hilt sticking out of his chest. It was till humming, as if it had a vicious mind of its own and suddenly, Lee felt the pain of its passage.

Looking at his soldiers, he gasped, "Let the dogs bite!" and, before he fell dead, he heard rather than saw the gunfire that riddled Roger's already dying body with bullets.

As porch lights around the neighborhood lit up, the *boo how doy* sawed Billy's head off and ran back to the second carriage. Then, they shot Pete Meadows full of holes, decapitated him and ran away as fast as they could into the first rays of early dawn.

46

"Dad…Dad!"

Matthew heard his son's words but didn't know what his boy was saying until Chance shook him roughly by the shoulder. "Pa! You gotta get up!"

Matthew started. *Dad* – another one of those new-fangled expressions Chance had picked up at the academy. *Dad,* Americanized from the Irish- *Da*…a nickname for father.

"Oh, Chance," Matthew groaned. "I screwed up so bad. I don't know how you can even look at me."

Chance took Matthew by the arm and hauled him to his feet. Shaking his head, he said. "Pa, I know you didn't want to give Chin Lee the satisfaction of looking up at him in the end, but I did…"

Matthew stared at Chance, and then murmured, "Yeah, so?"

Chance rolled his eyes. "So, he winked at you…winked! And when you refused to look up at him, he winked at me. Don't you see? I think he was lying about Sweetie and

Steve. I might be wrong, but I think they're still alive. Come on, we gotta go see!"

Feeling a glimmer of hope, Matthew studied his son's face. If nothing else, his boy had a keen mind for one so young, and plenty of insight. Matthew said, "Okay, son. Prepare for the worst, but maybe you're right. Let's go!"

They passed a few people as they crossed the yard and at one point, Matthew heard a man say, "Yup, the man's head was cut clean off...what a sight!"

Stopping, Matthew asked, "What man was that?"

The man looked over his shoulder and answered, "The one you shot, Mister. Kevin Woolsey. The doc wanted a look-see and when he saw what was left, he upchucked his own dinner!" The man burst into laughter, adding, "I don't care, though. Kevin was a bad hombre and I say good-riddance to bad rubbish!"

Matthew and Chance hurried on and stepped inside the Lucky Lady Saloon. To their absolute shock, Sweetie sat at one of the back tables, sucking a bloody thumb, and her friend Steven was rustling up a couple of drinks from the bar.

Sweetie was frowning and looked like she was trying not to cry. Matthew was so overjoyed he ran up, seized her in his hands and hugged her tight. "My God, Sweetie. You're alive! I thought...I thought you were dead!"

"No," she murmured against his chest, "just humiliated and sad, so sad about Edwin." The tears she'd been holding in check spilled from her eyes, and Matthew rocked her as she wept.

Steven brought two stout whiskeys to the table and Randall followed him with a pot of coffee and five empty cups. He was trembling and still grieving over the loss of his old friend. Steven smiled at Matthew as he sat down and said, "Randall found us tied up like Granny's prize pigs after those Chinese soldiers came."

Matthew shook his head. "Chin Lee told me that he killed you. I really thought..."

Sweetie sighed. "Interesting man, that Chin Lee. When he grabbed the pistol out of Steven's hand, I thought we were done for, and I grabbed my sword, but he plucked it away from me as quick as you please! The only thing I got for using it is a cut finger...self-inflicted, God help me!"

"So, what happened to Billy Drake and his boys, do you know?" Steven asked.

Matthew looked at the employees who were picking up the bar; the broken furniture, shattered mirrors, and rubble left over from Drake's goons, and saw that they were trying hard not to stare at the pretty lady sitting at the table. A woman named Sweetie Mack, who was, apparently, the principle owner rather than the young man they knew as Martin Mercer.

He shook his head. "I honestly don't know, but I don't think it was anything good. Before he and his soldiers left, Lee said he needed to take Drake and his two top lieutenants back to Seattle to face the Tong leader's wrath. He also said he'd killed you both, so I don't know whether that was the truth, or another lie."

Chance spoke up. "Pa, I think it was the truth. I really think he told us he'd killed Sweetie and Steven for his soldiers' benefit. Or maybe the Tong leader in Seattle. At any rate, Billy, Pete and Kevin are gone...well," he paused, "part of Kevin is still here, I guess."

Sweetie looked back and forth between Matthew and his son and asked, "What does *that* mean?"

"I shot Kevin Woolsey, Sweetie. He was raping a girl, and I lost my temper. Still, sometime over the last half-hour or so, his head went missing. The Tong probably has it... they're into that kind of thing."

Sweetie's shoulders sagged again, and she said, "I still can't believe Edwin is gone..." Tears spilled from her eyes, and Randall put his small, bony arm around her shoulders. Matthew could hear him whisper, "He loved you, my girl, and died doing what he loved to do."

Sweetie nodded and sniffed away her tears. Then, looking up she saw a number of policemen enter the bar along with three tall men wearing silver stars on their low-crowned hats.

"Ah, the U S Marshals are here, at last," Matthew said. Standing up, he made his weary way to the front of the saloon to give his account of the trouble surrounding The Lucky Lady Saloon.

Epilogue

About eight months later, Matthew and Chance Wilcox stepped off the train in Wenatchee, Washington. It was a cool and rainy February afternoon, snow still clinging to tree branches and the sides of the road.

Looking past the working trains, Matthew noticed that the little Chinatown by the railroad siding seemed to have diminished since he was last here, and he thought he knew why. He had been following the U.S. Marshals' and the Pinkertons' investigation into Billy Drake and the Tong religiously.

As soon as the local police and the Marshals had walked in the door of The Luck Lady Saloon that fateful night last June, their investigations began. The first thing the cops did was go to Billy Drake's mansion where they found Billy, his second in command, Pete Meadows and the Tong lieutenant, Chin Lee, murdered and headless in front of the house.

There was another dead body on the lawn, as well; a

fellow named Roger Hampsted, who had worked for Drake as a henchman and general roustabout. He was shot full of holes but apparently, his head was deemed unimportant. Upon further investigation by the local doctor, the man was already half-dead from some previous altercation, his body riddled with sepsis, and half his organs shut down.

The Pinkertons had moved swiftly. They were no strangers to the Tong, and the gangs' habit of using decapitated heads for identification. A number of Pinks and Marshals simply boarded trains and postal wagons and followed the heads back to Seattle's Chinatown.

They had found those noggins, minus one, in a lavish mansion on Nob Hill, but the home's occupants had fled by the time they arrived. Apparently, the Tong leader known as Zhang Wei had uprooted his family and fled north into Canada.

As far as Matthew knew, further investigation into Zhang Wei and his soldiers was stymied for now, but the Pinkertons were requesting a suspension of political asylum from the Canadian government which, rumor had it, was coming soon. After all, the Tong were dangerous, and the officials in Vancouver B.C. were as nervous as cats on a wet fence since the gangs' arrival.

One thing became clear, though. The missing head, Chin (Lucky) Lee's, was found in the possession of an old Chinese woman in a carriage en route to California. The marshals who found her said she surrendered most of her possessions without complaint, until they tried to take the box containing her son's earthly remains, which stunk like a charnel house.

Upon investigating the box's contents, they found a note written in Chinese. According to their interpreter, the note read; *All debts are paid in full.* The marshals held the old woman captive for a while, hoping to glean more information from her, but she was clearly distraught and only desired to join her daughter's family in San Francisco.

After a couple of weeks, the woman was released, clutching only a small suitcase and an old cracked teapot to her chest, as she left.

As for Billy Drake and his gang, there was nothing left of them but the crying. Many of Billy's gang were dead, and those that were left were cooling their heels in jail. After hearing of Drake's death, witnesses came en mass to testify about his numerous crimes, from far in the past to the present day.

Rape, murder and too many thefts to count were laid at Billy's dead feet. After learning that their mayor and many of the cops in his employ were nothing more than criminals, the people of Wenatchee rose up in anger, and stormed the jailhouse to exert their own brand of citizen justice, but the U.S. Marshals stepped in and stopped innocent folks from sullying their own good names in an illegal lynching.

In all the hubbub, though, one thing became clear. Many of Drake's former employees stated that Billy's safe was filled with cash, and the Pinkertons brought in their own safecracker to open the metal box. It was a stout, double-reinforced safe but eventually it was opened to reveal a fortune in gold, silver and cash notes.

The Pinks claimed their share, as did the U.S. Marshals, but most of the cash was given back to the many victims of Billy's crimes. A lot of the money went to old Clive Hancock, some was rewarded to the Stine brothers, along with their own bar, and the rest went to Drake's victims, both past and present.

Tom (The Black Cat) was one of the recipients, and so was Sweetie Mack. They were awarded money to rebuild, but they had declined the compensation. Matthew and Chance were about to find out why.

The fog and rain had lifted by the time they pulled in front of the Lucky Lady Saloon. Looking around, Matthew smiled. The place had really changed, and all to the good.

A small but pretty house had been built behind the restaurant, and the saloon itself had almost doubled in size. The barnyard was bigger, and a garden had been cut into the landscape which, according to Sweetie's letters, would be plenty big enough to supply the restaurant and half the valley with all the produce it could possibly use.

The biggest change to the landscape was a new smithy, horse barn and general store. In front of the general store hung a sign that read, Mayoral Office-ANDREW FORSYTHE, Mayor.

A huge figure emerged from the smithy, and Chance hollered, "Hey, Tommy! Long time, no see!" Matthew's son hopped from the carriage and ran to shake hands with his friend. At the same moment, Sweetie stepped out onto the front porch, and waved.

Matthew grinned and noted the slight bulge in her belly underneath the apron she wore. *So,* he thought, *the rumors are true! Sweetie and Tom had gotten married on the sly and were expecting a baby!*

Sweetie's hair had grown out by now, her round blue eyes were twinkling, and her cheeks were flushed with happiness. Matthew marveled as she ran up to him with open arms and thought, *it's amazing how love can cure even the most broken soul!*

A few moments later Tom reached them, and Matthew watched as the two young lovers fell into each other's arms, as close and tight as new magnets and joyful in their union.

At that point many citizens spilled out the front doors, and trays of food were walked outside to feed the folks who'd come to welcome him and his son back to town. A small band of local musicians started warming up in the backyard and Matthew realized that Tom and Sweetie were throwing a party on their behalf.

Even as he and Chance were swept away by their happy hosts, Matthew couldn't help but remember his own history and heartbreak, and hope that maybe, someday, he too would find peace and love.

Then, before Matthew could succumb to the ever-present grief of losing his wife, Sweetie seized his hand and he found himself dancing the latest Dosido.

A Look At The Pistol Man's Apprentice

Scarred by the Civil War, now a loner by choice, Missouri-born Jack Ballard rides the West in search of trouble. Sometimes he's able to stop it from hurting innocent people—and sometimes he causes it.

It can't be helped, though. He is a good man with a fast gun, and in West Texas in the late 1800's, trouble lies around every bend.

Only he and his filed-down .44-40 Colt can stop it.

AVAILABLE NOW

ABOUT THE AUTHOR

Linell Jeppsen is a writer of science fiction and fantasy. Her vampire novel, Detour to Dusk, has received over 44- four and five star reviews. Her novel Story Time, with over 130 4-and 5-star reviews, is a science fiction post-apocalyptic novel, and has been touted by the Paranormal Romance Guild, Sandy's Blog Spot, Coffee time Romance, Bitten by Books and 64 top reviewers as a five-star read, filled with terror, love, loss, and the indomitable beauty and strength of the human spirit. Story Time was also nominated as the best new read of 2011 by the PRG. Her dark fantasy novel, Onio (a story about a half-human Sasquatch who falls in love with a human girl), was released in December 2012 and won 3rd place as the best fantasy romance of 2012 by the PRG reviewers guild. Her novel, The War of Odds, won the IBD award for fantasy fiction and boasts 18 5-star reviews since its release in February of 2013. It also placed 2nd, as the best YA paranormal book of 2013 by the PRG.

CPSIA information can be obtained
at www.ICGtesting.com
Printed in the USA
LVHW032033251120
672678LV00006B/1289